HIS LITTLE STAR

MICHELLE KARISE

This book is for the starry-eyed girls with
hearts as big as the sky.

Close your eyes and make a wish.

HIS LITTLE STAR

CHAPTER ONE

Naomi

"**C**all me when you land."

The email was short and to the point. Coming from my father, it could've meant just about anything from "*I want to go over the plan with you one more time to make sure you don't screw it up,*" to "*The sewer backed up and exploded all over the hotel, and we're about to go under,*" or even "*What kind of flowers does your mother like again?*" Perhaps some words of encouragement, as his precious little girl had, once again, made him proud.

I prepared myself for the worst. When it came to my father, business trips were just that—business. From the moment I landed in Rome until the minute I took off for New York City, I'd be on the clock. In his eyes, at least. Ephraim Jackson didn't take breaks, and as his daughter, I was expected to adhere to the same philosophy. Most of the time, we saw things eye to eye. However, I also understood all work and no play made for a rather tense Naomi.

A girl could have some fun, right?

For the sake of my father's peace of mind, I would keep that bit to myself.

That being said, his email had me all kinds of curious. What did he have to say over the phone that he couldn't have explained in a text message?

I'd worked for the hotel division of Cygnus Group for two years. In that short period, I'd learned the difference between my father and my boss. My father was funny and a good husband. My boss was a hard-nosed executive with a take-no-prisoners leadership approach. He possessed a sharp mind for contracts and used loopholes to finagle himself out of weak agreements. I took notes and aimed to be like him.

The familiar ding of the jet's intercom system sounded. The captain's deep voice boomed through the speakers. "Ladies and gentlemen, this is Captain Anderson. We're about to make our descent into beautiful Rome, Italy. The weather is a balmy seventy-two degrees Fahrenheit, or twenty-two degrees Celsius, with not a cloud in the sky. Flight attendants, please prepare the cabin for landing."

I finished off my distilled water before handing the glass to the flight attendant. I tucked away my laptop, fastened my seat belt, and relaxed in the plush leather seat.

Perfect.

Twenty minutes later, the plane was on the ground and taxiing to Ciampino International Airport's private aviation terminal. When we came to a complete stop, I whipped out my phone and toggled from airplane mode. Before I could even dial, my father's name showed up on the screen.

"Do you have ESP?" I teased, a smile playing on my lips.

"I've been tracking your flight." His tone was all business. I imagined him standing in his office, looking out the floor-to-ceiling windows with one hand on his hip and the other tightly clutching the phone. He likely had a clenched jaw and barely controlled irritation blazing in his eyes. "We've got a problem."

Four words I always dreaded coming from my father. The *we* in his statement meant *me*, and the problem would blow a hole in the plans I'd made for the next few weeks.

"I'm eager to solve it," I said confidently.

Twenty-six years of being his daughter had taught me to respond to his heightened emotional state with an equal amount of coolness. That seemed to keep his emotions from spiraling out of control. My ability to be the "executive whisperer" was the reason I quickly became one of his most trusted advisors.

I looked down at my feet and released a low sigh. I wished he'd have been a bit kinder and more appreciative of my hard work.

"My assistant informs me that the locals have organized a protest outside the hotel property."

I snorted. "Since when has that been a concern?" I scrunched up my nose. "Unless they're getting violent. Am I about to be pelted with vegetables?"

"No one does that anymore." Impatience permeated

his voice, a signal that perhaps this wasn't the time to turn on the charm.

"Tell that to my coat that got stained from a tomato in Nice." I let out a huff of agitation.

Generally, the local townspeople's protests were verbal and rarely became violent. The locals hated change, and then once it arrived, they sang a different tune. We'd saved communities with the increase in tourism we'd created.

Ignoring my witty remarks, my father got to the point. "This protest is about to get complicated in other ways. It has a wealthy supporter who isn't hesitating to involve the entire town to get his way. The kicker: he's a hotel owner himself."

"He's scared."

"Yes. There's a meeting scheduled with this man tomorrow to find a compromise that will get his supporters to back down. It'd be nice not to have to jump through all the legal hoops again."

"We won't open in time if that's the case."

"Precisely, and our VIP guests coming for the grand opening will be disappointed if they have to adjust their travel plans because of petty jealousy. The administrative team will bring you up to speed on the protest organizer. Don't go in cold; the guy's tenacious. Be sure to do your own research before the meeting."

I nodded out of habit and got up from my seat so I could gather my work bag. "Don't worry. I've got this covered. Whoever this guy is, I'll have him eating out of the palm of my hand by the end of our meeting."

"You're a gem, my dear. Please be careful."

"Thank you, Daddy." I flashed a grin in response to the unexpected endearment. It felt like the good old days—before the pressures of work had changed our relationship. "I'll give you all the brutal details afterward."

I gripped my laptop bag and exited the plane, the widest of smiles on my lips. Many men had feared the type of conquest before me and had buckled under the pressure. I wasn't a man, though, and I immensely enjoyed some good old-fashioned boardroom carnage.

CHAPTER TWO

Matteo

"There needs to be more protestors in front of the hotel. They should be there twenty-four hours a day—not just during the daylight." Anger twisted through my body, tying me into knots.

My office space inhabited the top floor of my hotel, Hotel Vesta Roma. Located in the Fourteenth Quarter, the view was one of Roma's best. On a clear day, a landscape of hills, stonework, and the Vatican could awe the most discriminating of travelers. The view was the reason guests returned time and time again. But on that day, I looked out my window and saw nothing but red.

"Sir, the protestors must make a living. They limit their hours to before work and a few hours in the afternoon," my assistant, George, said, his voice sheepish and barely audible through the receiver.

Raucous jeers and boos rang from the other end of the call. One of George's responsibilities was to support the protestors. Each day, he stopped by the front lines to ensure there was plenty of water and fruit.

I scratched at my beard as I considered his statement. "You are correct. We can't give Ephraim Jackson the pleasure of comfort during this trip."

"Jackson's still in the United States."

I tightened my grip on the armrest of my chair. "That arrogant *bastardo*! So confident he will get his way that he cannot be bothered to face me like a man!"

"Your meeting will be with another senior officer instead."

I let out a heavy breath. "Fine, although I won't get as much joy from destroying the man he has sent in his place."

It figured Jackson would avoid meeting with me in person. For three years, I'd been a thorn in the side of the city council and by default, Ephraim Jackson and Cygnus Group. The man was a bit of a coward with a fondness for sarcasm-laced emails. He only walked into fights he knew he could win and left the rest of the actual work to his staff.

George was silent for a few seconds. My assistant was far too gentle for the world of business. I could sense his fear. When I spoke next, it was far more calmly than I felt. "Thank you, Georgio—forgive me—*George*, for the update. I appreciate it. Please learn more about the person we'll be meeting, and we'll discuss your findings in the morning. Keep me informed if any additional changes to the agenda should occur."

"Yes, sir. You're welcome." He hung up, no doubt relieved

he was no longer on the receiving end of my frustration. I hadn't intended to take it out on him. At the same time, he had a long way to go if he expected to make it in the business world. Most bosses wouldn't be so kind as to even think of his feelings.

Most bosses wouldn't take a twenty-three-year-old under their wing and teach him all there was to know about business. We had similar upbringings—orphaned at a young age and raised by our grandmothers. When I met Georgio, he lacked direction but had a strong desire to learn. I'd supported him throughout university, and after graduation, I gave him a job as my personal assistant.

I sat back in my chair and put my feet up on my desk. Staring off into space, I waited until my heart rate sufficiently decreased and my anger dissipated.

Alone with my thoughts and now calm, I was able to develop the next best course of action. Whomever the senior officer was, I would have to find a way to persuade him to see things from my perspective. Jackson's hotel could *not* open. I didn't want to have to play dirty, although I would to win. I had to win. Jackson didn't understand the community in which he wanted to do business, and he certainly wasn't worthy of stepping foot in this town—let alone owning a stake in it.

The rage building inside of me at the mere mention of his name was enough to create fantasies of punching him in the face. Who knew what seeing him in person might spark.

Calm down, Matteo. He isn't worth such a strong reaction.

I could practically hear my grandmother's voice in my head. Years had gone by since her passing, yet I still remembered what she sounded like as clear as day.

I took in a few slow breaths. Tomorrow, I would deal with the inconvenience of Ephraim Jackson. Until then, I knew just how to let off some steam.

CHAPTER THREE

Naomi

A luxury sedan took me from the airport to the new hotel. The entrance to the property was just as grand as the other properties in our portfolio. A blend of classic Roman architecture and modern amenities made for one of our most elegant buildings yet.

I was there to observe operations and make tweaks to improve service. I would be the only guest at the hotel as we were tying up loose ends with construction and training.

Item one on my checklist: Ensure first impressions meet company standards. *Complete!*

As Chief Experience Officer, my job was to examine the quality of just that—customer experiences on our properties. Guests paid good money to be treated like royalty for the duration of their stay. I had the tough job of letting the staff show me how well they took their tasks to heart. Were the Swedish massages administered with light or medium pressure? Were the drinks crafted with care? What was the chlorine count in the pools? How energetic was the personal trainer? All those items and more were on my list.

I also got to rub elbows with VIP guests and investors. And put out any small fires that might arise to delay progress—like the protestors who had been standing outside the property lines.

A tall, slender man with an impeccably groomed mustache opened the car door. I pulled my knees together and swung my legs to the ground. I took his extended hand as he helped me out of the car. His smile was warm and welcoming—I ticked off another box on my checklist.

"*Signorina* Martin, your room is ready for you," The man wore a name tag that read "Salvatore." Below his name was his title, General Manager, written in English and Italian.

I used my mother's maiden name professionally. Doing so cut down on the gossip that my father had placed me in this cushy executive position because I was his only child. Also, I'd learned that staff and clients respected my suggestions and decisions when they weren't reminded of my relationship to their boss.

For the time being, I ignored him and admired the glass doors leading inside. "Bright and clean. Good."

"Y-yes?" He didn't seem to understand.

I looked over at him and gave him my famous business smile. The one that made it impossible to tell how I felt. Was I happy or angry? Was I impressed or displeased? No one knew, and that would make him and the rest of the staff edgy for the duration of my stay. Testing who thrived or broke under pressure was vital to the success of the hotel. Our employees needed to be comfortable turning tough customers into return customers. Each interaction with a staff member was an opportunity for me to identify weakness and provide on-the-spot performance feedback.

"Please bring my things up for me. I'm going to take a walk around the grounds," I told him before making my way to the door.

He stood there for a second and then dashed ahead to open the glass doors for me. "Of course. I'm happy to give you a tour."

"A guided tour isn't necessary. We have our formal walkthrough scheduled for tomorrow. This will be nothing more than a glance." I batted my eyelashes at him.

"As you wish," he answered in an even tone with a courteous smile that didn't reach his eyes. He turned to the bellhop and made a subtle wave for the young man to unload my luggage. "If there is anything you need—"

"I will be sure to let you know." I gave him a polite nod before pressing onward.

Exploring the grounds on my own gave me the time and space I needed to unwind from the plane ride. I saw the hotel through the same lens as an arriving guest—travel weary but with an appreciation of the luxurious surroundings. Did I mention it gave me space? For the duration of my stay, Salvatore and the rest of the staff would continuously check on my comfort level and ensure my every whim was taken care of, lest I report back that their hospitality was not up to Cygnus Group standards.

I walked through the lobby to a courtyard filled with lavish local flowers. The sun shone onto my face, and I took in a deep, cleansing breath before sliding on my designer sunglasses. It was probably one of the few *me* moments I'd get while at the hotel.

My evening was going to be comprised of a long bath and much-needed rest. It had been a long day, and there was nothing I needed more than time to decompress. I sat on a bench and pulled out my phone. Within seconds, my mother's face filled the screen.

Josephine Martin-Jackson was affectionately known as Josie. Twenty-eight years ago, she'd moved from Middle America to New York City in hopes of becoming a fashion model. After hundreds of open calls that went nowhere, she'd been ready to return to Kansas City. One evening, an enterprising man who had nothing more than a risk-taking spirit and a dream ate at the diner where she worked. My father had sat at one of her tables, and by the end of the evening, she'd had his number and a date. The rest, as they say, was history.

"Hi, sweetheart. How's my baby girl?" My mother's warm, soft voice flowed through the receiver. She'd come a long way from her life in Missouri. With skin the color of chestnut, she was elegant with her chin-length bob and tastefully age-appropriate makeup. She wasn't a socialite but was popular in the charitable community. She was a trustee for the Metropolitan Museum of Art and volunteered at a childcare center in her spare time.

No matter my age, I would always be my mother's baby girl. When I was a teenager, I'd hated the term of endearment with a fiery hot passion, but as I got older, I didn't mind as much.

"Hi, Mom. I arrived safely and had a few minutes, so I wanted to check in before things get hectic. The hotel is gorgeous." I turned the camera around and panned the courtyard before turning it back.

"It's lovely. So, what are your plans while you're there?" She moved closer to the camera, her entire face filling the screen.

"Training for the grand opening."

My eyes drifted back to the garden. I understood the intent behind her question. She didn't understand the reasons my work was important. I couldn't explain the sense of accomplishment after a hard day's work. Five-star guest reviews were the motivation to up my game and come up with innovative ideas.

"You work too hard. Stop it. I would like you to take a few moments and see the sights. Life will pass you by if you don't stop and smell the flowers." I smiled when she let out a small laugh.

"How about this? I'll pick up a few bottles of lavender-infused Limoncello. When I return, we'll get a nice charcuterie board and hang out on the rooftop deck."

"I'm going to hold you to it." There was a tiny glint of excitement in her gaze.

"Mom, I gotta go. I love you."

"Love you, too." She blew a kiss before hanging up.

Mom had given me the right idea. I should take in the sights. *All the more reason to not spend all my time at the hotel, right?*

Day one always had a minimal agenda—arrive, refresh, prepare. I mentally took plenty of notes on my first impressions, sure, but I wouldn't scrutinize too harshly until the morning. The staff got a few hours of reprieve, a chance to resolve their nervous jitters before I took them to task. If they knew I was doing them this favor, they'd have thanked me. A wound-up Naomi only amplified the *bitch* part instead of the *boss* part.

Life's stresses often built up as tension in my neck and shoulders, and at that moment, there was a dull throb at the top of my spine. There were many ways to siphon off tension. Some people enjoyed hot baths and practiced meditation, whereas others liked vigorous exercise.

Lucky for the staff, I knew just how to let loose. It'd been a while since I'd been laid, and it was long overdue.

I sensed Salvatore standing nearby—waiting just in case I needed him. And I did.

"Where's the best nightclub near here?"

CHAPTER FOUR

Matteo

Many of my peers wouldn't imagine a man of my prominence would go to such an establishment. There were quieter, more discreet clubs—those made especially for men of my age for the sole purpose of finding a young and eager beauty to impress. The kind of club for older men to feel young and be lied to about their sexual prowess. Not my kind of place. Did I stand out? Yes, and I used that to my advantage and then proved how well I could keep up on the dance floor as well as in the bedroom.

Toyland nightclub was a carnival dedicated to sexiness. There were beautiful bodies as far as the eye could see. Scantily clad women danced in gilded cages. Couples dry humped in the corners while multi-colored fluorescent lights illuminated their heaving figures.

Cloaked by the crowd of revelers, I stood at the edge of the bar and sipped on my negroni. I watched the scene surrounding me. Four twentysomething blonde women bounced to the music, knowing full well their braless breasts would grab plenty of attention. Attractive? Yes. Exciting? No. They looked like every cliché university student traveling through Europe. Hardly any fun. I'd done that song and dance a few times. We'd laughed, had a great time, but I'd always left looking for… more.

Perhaps it was optimistic of me to go to a club in search of a woman who might challenge me. Stranger things had happened. That said, I had no problem with biding my time, either. I enjoyed casual sex as long as my heart stayed turned off—no harm, no foul. A night with one of the blondes? I could do better.

And that was precisely when "better" walked through the door.

From across the room, a beautiful woman glided across the floor wearing a sheath of a dress on her hourglass figure and heels accentuating her long legs. I watched her with interest because I'd never seen her before. It was hard to ignore the way the light danced on her brown skin and those dark, luscious curls. More importantly, the confidence she used to survey the room. She was a woman who knew what she wanted and wouldn't settle for less.

Every male stare landed on her, each man mesmerized by the swing of her hips as she walked to the bar. My primal instincts reared up, pumping competitive adrenaline through my veins. She was mine and I would beat back anyone who dared to challenge me.

Two people separated me from the beauty. I watched as she nodded a greeting to our neighbors, then studied the liquor lining the wall. She raised a finger to signal a bartender.

A challenge, and I was happy to accept it.

CHAPTER FIVE

Naomi

Toyland was one of Rome's oldest nightclubs. It was a subterranean space filled with good-looking people, alcohol, and blaring music. Under the glow of LED lighting, scores of partyers filled the dance floor, pumping their fists and their bodies.

As I bypassed the entry line into the club and let the music blasting from inside envelope me, I let my inner queen out. She was eager to find a loyal subject and make him bow.

For a moment, I took in the atmosphere, and disappointment wafted over me when I realized I was in a regular nightclub.

What kind of woman did Salvatore think I was? I didn't want the ordinary. I liked speakeasies, underground sex clubs, and dungeons—places where I could experience the unexpected.

Of course, he couldn't know. He'd recommended a location he'd thought was appropriate for a visitor.

However, I could mix a little work with pleasure. It

might be fun to pretend to be a typical tourist and see the local flavor from that angle. Many of our clientele would find their way to this club. If the ambiance was unsuitable for our guests, that gave me the chance to lecture the staff about making sure they only recommended the best of the best.

We'd see how well Toyland stacked up.

The girls on the dance floor appeared to be having the time of their lives. Not far away was the bar, and a drink sounded appealing after the day I'd had. I sashayed over that way, letting the music move my hips. I might not have been the same age as the dancing blondes, but we shared the same vibes—time to let my hair down and have some fun.

As I contemplated my drink of choice, I caught the gaze of a man standing a few feet away. He'd tried to be inconspicuous, but his manliness was impossible to hide. He watched my every move. His graying temples and smile lines gave away his age, but despite clearly being older than I was and wearing a suit, he fit in with the crowd just fine. *How intriguing.* This was a guy who put a whole new meaning to the Roman conquest, and it looked like he'd chosen me as his next territory to invade.

His first wave of attack—holding onto my gaze with his own as he made his way over to me. Each step he took had a confidence and swagger that only a man of experience could master. Usually, I didn't find arrogance attractive. If he were any other man, I'd have narrowed my glare and sent him into a cowardly retreat. This man… hot damn. I didn't want to say no. His victory wouldn't be an easy one, though.

"*Buonasera.* I hoped I'd catch you before you ordered a drink." The smile he gave me wasn't smug. He spoke to me as though we'd known each other for years. I couldn't quite figure out his angle. There should have been some kind of smooth pickup line.

I faced him and stared into his deep, dark eyes. An inexplicable feeling came over me; we were physically close, but I wanted him closer. His hand hovered over the small of my back, and I wished he'd close the gap so I could feel the heat of his skin against mine. *Why tease me?*

I couldn't let my eagerness show just yet. "Is that your way of offering to buy me a drink?"

He raised both of his eyebrows, surprise filling his voice. "You're an American." He moved in closer. "Would you accept such an offer?"

"That depends on what strings are attached. I'm assuming it's not a gift, but rather an invitation," I said nonchalantly.

His eyes narrowed for a moment before softening as he chuckled. "*Stellina,* only to dance, I promise."

Should things go beyond that, though… were the words he left unsaid.

"Accepting the drink is not a transaction," he added. "By all means, walk away, throw it in my face, do as you please."

That piqued my curiosity. Few men would dare suggest such a thing. After all, the whole point of buying a drink was to launch the first strike. "What would you call this offer then?"

"Hope." He leaned in, his voice growing low and seductive. "Desire. I wouldn't deceive you into thinking my motives are pure—far from it. I want you. In my bed. Most importantly, I want you there because the idea of keeping your hands off me kills you inside." Slowly, he pulled back. "Not because of transactions."

And there it was—the pickup line.

I swallowed, taking in his words. Arrogant *and* honest. "No tantrum if I refuse?"

I carefully studied his features under the nightclub lights. His full, kissable lips led to a Romanesque nose framed by high cheekbones. A quiet lust simmered beneath the surface as he locked eyes with mine.

Panty dropper. There really was no other way to describe this man. This wasn't a case of gin goggles. He was a bona fide hottie.

My attraction intensified under his stare. My legs turned to jelly. I needed to stabilize myself, or I would end up sprawled on the floor.

"Do not mistake me for one of the boys here." He made a vague wave toward the younger men in the room. "I'll be disappointed, but I promise I will let you leave in peace."

I trailed a few fingers into his dark hair and twisted a stray curl around them gently. "Why don't you stick around for a while and keep me company?"

"I've had my eyes on you since you entered the room," he said with a wink.

"Listen, you don't have to lay it on thick," I said, adding a flirtatious laugh. "You had me at *buonasera*."

His lips spread into a dazzling smile. "But it is true. I have a taste for only beautiful things."

A blush warmed my cheeks, an uncharacteristically girlish reaction to his compliment. The stranger had me on edge. *Get it together, Naomi. No matter how alluring this man is, be cautious with your emotions.*

I stood straighter, squared my shoulders, and took a sip from my glass. It was all a vain attempt to prepare myself for what would surely be an intense roll in the sack.

He watched my movements with curiosity before he introduced himself at last. "Matt."

"Naomi," was all I offered. No need for last names or more details. We both knew exactly how this night was going to end.

Matt and I finished off our drinks and headed to the dance floor. The alcohol in my drink had filled me with warmth, lubricating my joints as I performed a slow hip roll. He moved behind me, his hands settling on my waist, matching his rhythm to mine.

"You are so sexy," he breathed against my ear.

We were a perfect fit, my curves aligned tightly against his hard body. The air in the club thickened as his pelvis ground against my ass. Eyes closed, I raised my arms and snapped my fingers along with the beat.

The DJ switched to a slower song. I twirled to face Matt and wrapped my arms around his muscular form. Resting my face on his chest, I took in deep inhales of him. I would never forget how he smelled. Woodsy with a hint of citrus and all male.

He ran his nose along my throat. That along with the low sound he made as he hummed along with the song was my undoing.

"My driver's outside. Why don't we get out of here?" he asked.

I jumped at the unexpected heat coming from his mouth as he whispered in my ear. For several beats, we stared at each other as we swayed to the music.

"Where? I don't feel comfortable going to my hotel." I stopped moving, but I still held on to him.

"My hotel's not far from here. I have a suite."

So, he was also a tourist. What luck! He was the perfect choice. It increased our chances of never bumping into each other again.

"Okay."

CHAPTER SIX

Matteo

After we finished our dance, I offered Naomi my arm and we walked out of the nightclub. Leaning onto each other, we glided across the cobblestone sidewalk to the street where my car awaited.

"The hotel, please," I said to the driver. He nodded, opening the door.

Once cocooned in the leather interior, I draped an arm around Naomi's shoulders and pulled her close. Her eyes were at half-mast, a glimmer of hunger there. The flash of streetlights streaked across her face, alternately showing and hiding her lovely features. Her eyelashes were thick and dark, framing eyes that twinkled like stars at night.

She was enchanting, and I was pleased that there was so much heat between us.

I placed my hand on her cheek, and she leaned into it, a small smile forming on her pretty face. Electricity sparked as I brushed my thumb over her mouth—so full and so soft. She closed her eyes, practically whimpering as I stroked her.

My heart thrummed loudly with anticipation. I couldn't wait to feel her long, lovely legs wrapped around my waist and her honey-soft breasts pressed against my bare chest.

On a sigh, Naomi shifted onto my lap. "Matt…" she drawled, running her tongue along her lips.

I winced. *Matt* was the name I gave women when I was out and about. I hated that I couldn't share my real name, but anything long term was not what we were there for.

Her mouth hovered over mine, warm breath misting my lips. She smelled like my beloved Amarena cherries that had been soaked in gin and Campari—a perfectly crafted cocktail oozing sex and confidence.

She moved in closer and closer until our lips touched. Her kiss rocked me to my toes, sending flames of heat to my extremities and pumping hot lava to my cock.

She was a gorgeous kisser. She quickly submitted to my control and permitted me to lead her through the kiss. In return, I took my time sliding my fingers through her curls and tangling my tongue with hers.

Her arms slipped around my neck, and she buried her fingers in my hair, clawing at my scalp. We continued to kiss until the car came to a complete stop in front of my hotel.

She slid off my lap and looked out the window to the hotel entrance. A slight frown gathered on her face before fading. "The Hotel Vesta. Very swanky."

I stepped out of the car and extended my hand. We moved through the revolving door and entered the reception area. She looked around, in awe of the indoor fountain, vivid colors, and the Tiffany-glass ceiling.

I tamped down the pride that swelled in my chest. An inexplicable familiarity existed between Naomi and me. Though we were as physically close as lovers, she could not know that I owned this hotel. In a few hours, she would leave, and we would never see each other again.

Enclosing her hand in mine, I led her to the bank of elevators. While we waited for one to arrive, I leaned in for another long, slow kiss.

We entered the waiting car and were whisked to one of the suites that I used for occasions like this. The atmosphere inside the elevator was thick with lust. The intoxicating blend of Naomi's floral perfume filled my senses and drew me in.

Once inside the suite, I flipped the light switch. Soft light filled the space, and the cooling system hummed. I pressed a button on the remote and sultry jazz echoed through the room. With her lips on mine, she wasted no time as she unbuckled my pants.

"Ah, *Stellina*, you go for what you want," I said, incredibly pleased. She wanted me, and who was I to deny her that pleasure?

She kissed along my jawline. "*Stellina*… What does that mean?"

"Little star. Your eyes are as brilliant as the stars above." The words were husky as they left my lips. Judging by the way she shivered, I knew they glided like silk to her core.

Naomi kissed me again, pulling me closer, practically clawing my clothing from my body, eager to scratch the itch only I could reach. I placed my hands over hers and used them to slow her down.

"Savor this, *Stellina*. Like a fine wine." I lavished her with kisses, beginning at her neck and slowly moving along her body, pulling her dress down as I went. I paused over each chocolate-drop nipple of her divine, perky breasts and suckled on them until she whimpered. Then I went lower… over her belly button. And lower, where I showed her just what I could do with my tongue and how I planned to savor *her*.

CHAPTER SEVEN

My body was restless with need. His teasing of every pleasure sensor I had was enough to drive me to the brink of no return yet hold me in agony because I wasn't *there* yet.

He trailed his hand down my belly, stroking the juncture of my thighs. He pulled aside the tiny strip of material that separated my delicate parts from the outside world and dipped his fingers inside, finding me indescribably wet. I softly moaned as he rubbed and stroked. My body bucked to the rhythm of his movements. He continued until my liquid pleasure dripped from his fingers.

Matt kneeled before me, burying his nose in my mound. He inhaled and expelled his breath with a rough, steady hiss. The sexy man pulled down my panties with his teeth. I moaned as he gently scraped the most sensitive parts of my body. He tossed the panties aside, hitched one of my legs over his shoulder, and dove in, kissing my soaked folds.

A rush of sensations hit me at once, making it

impossible to think. My body came alive with a desire I'd never felt before. I bit my lip and dug my nails into his shoulders to prolong riding out his massacre of my most secret spot.

His mouth spoke of decades of experience. He knew where to take me and how to get me there. My hands tangled in his hair as I cried and writhed in pleasure. Each lick and suck took me to new heights. He worked me well, but I needed more.

"How much longer are you going to make me wait?" I managed to ask, although I wanted to beg for him to just fuck me hard and fast. It wouldn't take much to get me to explode with pure ecstasy at the rate he was going. When he'd said he wanted me to savor the moment, I imagined nothing like this. I wanted nothing more than to arrive at my destination, yet also to keep it going... and going... and going. Like that damned rabbit from the battery commercials.

In response to my demand, he gave me the smirk of a challenge. "Are you not enjoying yourself?"

That's when I took things into my own hands. I also had plenty of experience. I guided Matt to his full height, slid closer to him, and slowly lowered his zipper. My hand sought his hardened shaft, and I proved he wasn't the only one who could be a tease. Wrapping my hand around him, I understood the source of his cockiness. He was a masterpiece—so thick and long. Arrogance filled me when he let out a quiet moan. I leaned in, whispering my fantasies as I gripped him, sliding across the length of his cock. Faster, with more need, I brought him right to the brink before letting him go. When he came, Matt erupted like Mount Vesuvius. His moans echoed inside the quiet room. His cum was thick like hot lava, splattering droplets on my hand and wrist.

He scooped me up into his arms, lifting me with little effort, and walked to the bedroom. He gingerly placed me on the mattress before pulling a wad of tissues from a box on the nightstand and gently wiping off my hand. He dropped his head, dipping his tongue between the seam of my lips. We kissed for an eternity as our hands explored each other's body, feeling every curve and muscle.

Matt was a virtuoso in seduction. His fingers nimbly removed the pins holding together the remains of my loose updo. The coils fell until they framed my face. As his body came back to life, his moans and whispers became sonatas composed only for me. I couldn't take any more; I needed to feel him.

"Fuck me, Matt. Do your worst."

He fucking growled—the deep rumble came from the pit of his soul and sent a river flowing from between my thighs. I freed his massive cock from its confines, gasping at its majesty. His thick dick pulsated with want. He grabbed a handful of condoms from the nightstand and frantically rolled one on. Without saying a word, he pushed me onto my back, moved over me, and plunged inside with one swift move. I bucked my hips toward him, our need equal as he went deeper and deeper. There was no escaping him, and it felt so… fucking… good. I cried out with each thrust. The swell of pressure traveled upward from the tips of my toes. My legs shuddered uncontrollably as my heart rate quickened. Every second I got closer until, at last, I reached that blissful moment surpassing all others.

And I felt satisfied, absolutely satisfied.

He kissed me softly before he pulled out and removed the condom.

Sweat glazed our bodies as we lay beside each other on the mattress, staring at the ceiling. Quiet for a moment, we lingered in the aftermath, relishing in it.

I rolled onto my side and glanced at him. So handsome and so hot. He turned to me and smiled. Time stood still as we stared at each other.

This was when one-night stands turned awkward. I wasn't sure what to say.

With a slight shake of his head, his expression became serious. "*Stellina*, there's water or champagne. Which would you like?"

"Water, please."

He rolled out of bed and walked to the living room. My gaze ate up his sculpted body. I admired his smooth movements and how his back muscles rippled down to his narrow waist. I took my time appreciating his firm ass and powerful legs. When he turned and walked back to the bed, the view from the front was even more impressive.

He trailed the frosty bottle against my arm. I yelped at the unexpected coldness.

The mattress shifted as he sat on the other side of the bed. We both untwisted the caps to our water and sipped from the bottles.

"So, what brings you to Rome?" I asked. I immediately wanted to crawl underneath the bed. I'd broken one of the cardinal rules of one-night stands—no personal questions. "I'm sorry. I didn't mean to pry."

He scooted down the mattress before rolling onto his side and propping his head on his hand. "*Stellina*, I would like to answer. I don't live far from here."

"Oh." I tried to hide the disappointment in my tone. He'd booked this room with the express purpose of having a one-night stand.

"You aren't happy with that answer. Let's change the subject. What brings you to Rome?"

"Business," I said flatly, taking another sip from the water bottle.

"Are you planning to sightsee?"

"No. Work takes up all of my time. I'll be surprised if I have time to catch dinner. I wanted to have one night of fun before I'm bogged down in meetings and training."

"*Stellina*, should you find time for yourself. I recommend going to a museum. The Galleria Borghese is the best choice for Italian art."

"I'll consider it. Thank you for the recommendation."

He reached out, taking a strand of my hair between his fingers. He wrapped the curl around his digit, gently pulling and watching it spring back. I smiled when he let out a small chuckle. He threaded his hand in the coils at the nape of my neck, pulling me closer until our mouths met.

Then he got serious.

The intensity of his gaze held me in place as he trailed a finger along my jaw. and laid his hand against my cheek. I sighed and leaned into his open palm. His thumb swiped over my mouth before dipping between my lips. Closing my mouth around the digit, I rolled my tongue around it. Both disappointment and excitement flashed through me as he removed his thumb and continued his descent down my neck to one of my nipples.

"Your nipples are so hard right now," he murmured. He traced my areola and tweaked my nipple. He moved closer, his mouth following along the path where his hand had been.

He cupped my breasts, his mouth closing over one of the mounds. "These beauties…" he whispered. His words were a groan filled with amazement.

Urging me onto my back, he scraped the stubble of his jaw against my sensitive nipples as he alternated his attention between my breasts—one peak and then the other. Gone was the frantic speed from earlier. He took his time, appreciating me.

He slowly rocked his pelvis against my hip. His cock sprang back to life, elongating and thickening with each thrust. I sought out his length and began a slow slide up and down.

Once satisfied that he was completely ready for me, I

nudged his shoulder until his back landed flat against the mattress. An uncontrolled fire blazed in his expression as I straddled him.

He grinned when I leaned over and pulled a gold foil packet from the nightstand. He brushed his fingernails along my arm, leaving a trail of goosebumps.

I ripped the latex from the package and slid it over him. Biting my lower lip, I held his cock flat against my cleft and shifted up and down. Eyes closed and head tilted back, I teased him, forcing him to beg for it.

"Mmm. Matt, your dick feels so good. Tell me what you want," I cooed.

"I want you…"

I held him as I painstakingly lowered onto his tip, hovering for a moment before I bore down on his cock. We both sighed as he bottomed out. I felt so full.

His hands landed at my waist—an encouragement to move. I slowly swiveled my hips as he released a long, guttural growl.

He looked up at me. "You're incredible."

I tried to hide my smug smile as I slid back and forth over him. Moving to his orchestrations, I rode him faster and faster. He slid his hand down and flicked at my nub. Electrical currents ripped through me as he pressed his thumb to my clit and began a small circle. With his other hand, he clamped onto my thigh and thrust up into me with an increasing rhythm.

My legs quaked. My pulse quickened as I raced to my

orgasm. I squeezed my eyes shut until black roses bloomed behind my eyelids.

His body shuddered before he spilled inside of me. He continued to pump, milking every drop he could give. When his dick softened, we carefully broke apart.

Damn. That was hot.

I leaned back against the pillow. Once I caught my breath, I would get dressed and make a hasty departure. I was caught by surprise when he wrapped an arm around me and held me against his chest. So much for an easy, clean escape.

No worries. I loved a good cuddle, and now that I was effectively spent, the jetlag was catching up. I'd indulge the gentleman, rest, and then leave before sunrise.

I'll just close my eyes for a few…

When I awakened from my nap, I blinked a few times, my vision hazy from sleep. The sun peeked through the crack of the curtains, its rays landing right on my face.

Wait… the sun!

I sat up with a start. Shit, I'd slept for too long. Staying the night implied I wanted more from Matt than I'd intended. It gave him control over the situation and an ego boost to boot. Although he deserved it. Because, damn, Matt had fucked me out of this galaxy. Thinking about the attentive way he'd worshiped the most sensitive places of my body had me tingling with anticipation all over again. *Calm down, greedy girl.* At least now, I had plenty of fantasies to entertain myself in the shower later.

Before I can play there, I need to get back to my hotel room.

A soft snoring sound reached my ears. I slowly crept out of bed, not wanting to wake him. Carefully, I tiptoed over to my panties. Just as I stepped into them, Matt's body shifted, and he cracked one eye open.

"*Stellina*, leaving so soon?" He flashed that smile that unleashed my inner queen, and I almost said, "*Fuck it all, let's go one more time…*"

But the clock said I had two hours until my morning meeting with the asshole trying to stop the hotel opening. I needed a shower—one that was distraction free!

He sat up against the headboard, and I got a good look at him in the daylight. The man was gorgeous… like Hollywood leading-man handsome. He ran a hand through his graying hair, sweeping back the stray strands and flexing his sun-bronzed biceps. My mouth gaped open as my gaze followed along his sculpted chest and down to his perfectly chiseled abs, where the sheets were arranged around his waist. Try as I might, I couldn't ignore the outline of his morning wood.

My mouth watered as I contemplated sticking around for another half hour, but my mind filled with images of my father's disapproving glare.

"I'm a busy woman. I have places to go and people to see." I flashed a smile back at him. "Thank you for a wonderful night."

"I'll call my driver. He'll take you where you need to go."

I shook my head. "Thank you, but that's not necessary. I'll manage."

He took my hand in his and brought it to his lips. "I hope we meet again."

"Yes," I said carefully. Oh, I wanted to see him again, too, but I had to be careful about how much of him I saw. Getting attached wouldn't end well for either of us.

After a moment's hesitation, I leaned in and kissed his cheek. "Thank you. That was lovely. Maybe we'll run into each other again."

There was so much hope in his goofy grin. *Wow, did I leave an impression on him!* And here I'd thought maybe he was just polite. Too bad I knew nothing about him.

The Hotel Vesta Roma was located a few blocks down the street from mine. As I exited the hotel, I looked up at the stone structure once more before taking the first steps of my stride of pride. While I'd enjoyed the sex, suspicion nagged and pulled at me. Something didn't feel right. The suit, the driver, and the luxury suite seemed excessive for a one-night stand.

There was a story there.

Was this the universe's way of telling me that I should run back to his suite and ask him to dinner? Or was it something else? Either way, there were other things to focus on other than a man I would likely never lay eyes on again.

I welcomed the walk back to my hotel. The fresh morning air would clear my head of that post-great-sex fog.

I walked into the hotel through the side door, made

my way upstairs to my suite, and took a nice, warm shower. From there, I dried off while wolfing down a giant bagel with cream cheese. Not the breakfast of champions, but I didn't have time to eat more.

Finally, I put on my power suit. The one with the sharp edges. It brought out the I-mean-business side of me the most. I paired the outfit with my favorite nude stilettos. I needed every advantage I could get going into this meeting. Not because I was facing an intimidating foe, but solely because I had to prove myself worthy of my position. Constantly.

That was fine, though. The more fight I got, the more fun I had.

CHAPTER EIGHT

Matteo

Naomi, *the beautiful young African American beauty.* I had chosen well last night.

Sinking into her had brought forth a cataclysm of sensations, sounds, and emotions. Her tight pussy had stretched and allowed me passage to sink deeply into her until we were pelvis-to-pelvis. She was heaven—a gift from God.

Last night, I held her tightly as we slept. My cock became a heat-seeking missile aimed at her naked, heart-shaped ass. I had remained a gentleman but had difficulty controlling him as he'd sought out and nestled in her warmth. At some point, I'd expected us to break apart and move to separate sides of the bed, but that didn't happen, and she'd stayed in my embrace the entire night. In less than a few hours, she'd taken control of both my mind and my body.

The morning light created a soft halo around her head. I marveled at her nude figure as she attempted to quietly gather her clothing and tiptoe out. Her firm, perky breasts and plump, round ass jiggled with each step, enticing me. It was all I could do to not pull her back into bed with me.

After blowing me a kiss, Naomi picked up her purse and sashayed out of the suite without a backward glance. The sound of the closing door echoed through the space, which left me alone with the quiet and my thoughts. The remnants of her feminine scent on my sheets were the faintest evidence of her existence. She'd exited my life as quickly as she'd entered, but not without leaving a mark.

For the first time in a long while, I felt satisfaction. When I told Naomi I hoped we'd meet again, I meant it. I never got to ask her last name, the name of her hotel, or how long she planned to stay in my city.

As I prepared for my morning meeting, I imagined how things would play out. I could look for her. That part wouldn't be complicated—I had plenty of staff skilled at researching the tourists in town. There were only so many places she could be staying. Our time together would be magnificent. We would part on such lovely terms. Perhaps she would invite me for a rendezvous the next time I traveled to America on business.

George greeted me in the hotel lobby. "Good morning, sir. We're meeting with one of Cygnus Group's officers."

"Did *Signor* Jackson change his mind?"

"No. We're meeting with the Chief Experience Officer. It's Martin, I think."

"You think?"

Brow furrowed, George scrolled through his phone as we walked to the bellhop area. "I didn't save my notes to the cloud. I'll run upstairs and grab my laptop."

"No. We don't have time. I'll wing it. If my offer to purchase isn't taken seriously, then we'll move to option two. We'll go after their restaurant and liquor licenses along with any permits."

We took the car down the street to the monstrosity Ephraim Jackson had built. To an untrained eye, it looked stunning. To my professional gaze, it was nothing more than generic. No heart in the design or appreciation for the land and her people.

We passed through the glass doors and entered what could only be considered a construction area. There were contractors buzzing about the lobby, making last minute touches to paint and installing light fixtures. A painter sanded a spot, forming a dust cloud. As luck would have it, white particles landed on my dark suit. I brushed at the sleeve of my jacket. This was one more annoyance to add to my list and fuel my anger.

"This Chief Experience Officer couldn't be bothered with greeting us at the door," I snarled as we rode the elevator up to the upper floor. "This site is filled with safety violations. I'll ask the legal team to add this to their list."

I rounded the corner leading to the meeting room. Through the entryway, I caught sight of a familiar profile. When the figure turned, curly sable locks swayed in front of her face and drew me to those captivating dark eyes from last night.

"Naomi," I whispered.

"Hmm? Yes, that's her name," George said. "How did you know?"

I narrowed my gaze at her and stalked into the room. "Pardon our lateness, *Stellina*."

Her entire body went rigid, and when she looked my way, I saw no trace of the fondness she'd shown me last night and this morning.

No, I saw wrath.

CHAPTER NINE

Naomi

"**M**att." His name left my lips like a curse. Honestly, he kind of was a curse. Attacking my business and trying to ruin my life, while at the same time being so fucking hot and knowing all the ways to make me moan. I hated that he knew how to do that, by the way. I didn't like that he'd had the pleasure of figuring it out in the first place. If I'd known who he was…

Don't lie to yourself, Naomi. You'd have still fucked him good.

There was great temptation to pull him to the conference table and win the argument by other methods. However, our colleagues might not appreciate such a… discussion.

I'd learned his identity shortly before he'd arrived. I hadn't been able to shake the suspicion that something wasn't right. My assistant presented me with a tablet that had more details. The short version was that Matt, otherwise known as Matteo Russo, was the president of the

Hotel Vesta brand. I'd pushed the tablet aside; just knowing he owned the property I'd visited last night was more than enough. Not only did I sleep with the enemy, but I did so on his turf.

I forced a smile and extended my hand. As Matteo and I shook hands, his grip was firm and warm. He held mine a little too long, and a dull throb between my legs served as a reminder of our shared secret. "Good morning. I'm Naomi Martin. Please, take a seat." I gestured to the chairs around the large conference room table. "Do you mind if I call you *Matt?*"

He studied me with interest, one side of his mouth ticked upward. Unbuttoning his jacket and he sat at one of the chairs surrounding the conference room table. "Yes, I mind. Please call me Matteo or *Signor* Russo."

"Let's talk." I sat down across from him and slid my business card across the table. "*Matteo*, it appears you have a problem with the location of Cygnus Group's newest addition."

His gaze brushed over me, lingering on my hair, my lips, and back to my eyes. Matteo squared his shoulders, such a typical power move. "I have many problems with the hotel. Location is just one of my concerns. I've taken my fight to the city council since they approved the rezone. The appeals were lost and ultimately denied."

"If the city rejected all the petitions, then you don't have a case," I said coolly.

"We're off on the wrong foot. I would like to redirect

this discussion. When Cygnus Group purchased the land, it was zoned residential. A few days after the papers were signed, the site was classified as commercial, without public comment or notice."

I stared at him blankly.

He continued. "My attorneys looked into the ordinances and filed the necessary paperwork to request a formal inquiry into the decision. It appears that the city council's actions did not follow the conventional procedure. There has been much corruption in the city government. I wanted to understand the urgency in the city council's actions."

"Matteo, I'm sure you understand that not every action requires a slow and languorous response. It's best to be quick. Nimble."

I thought back to his strong, purposeful thrusts. Each pump delivered so I wouldn't forget him or his magical cock.

A fire ignited in his stare, raising the temperature in the room by ten degrees. He leaned across the table, looking me straight in the eye. "Quick is never the appropriate response. Measured and deliberate moves are always better."

I drifted back to memories from hours ago. How he'd cried out my name using that same husky tone. I shifted in my chair and crossed my legs. He smiled when he saw the slight shift of my hips. He maddeningly raised a brow before he sat back in his seat.

Score one for Matteo.

"I like to speak facts. Cygnus Group legitimately acquired the land. We've complied with local rules and regulations regarding safety standards. We've incorporated green practices into our day-to-day operations. There's not much you can do at this point. We're proceeding with the hotel. If you'd like, I can give you a tour. You'll see that our brand of luxury is modern and on trend. Overstuffed furniture and rose-scented lobbies are a thing of the past. Perhaps I can give you a few pointers on modernizing your brand." I casually threw out the last sentence.

One point for me.

I waited for Matteo's response, surprised at how tightly he clenched his jaw.

"Miss Martin, there's nothing you can teach me." He took in a slow breath. "If Mr. Jackson had any decency, he would've responded to my purchase offer. He would be here so we could discuss the proposition face-to-face."

A purchase offer? I casually picked up the iPad and shifted through the project folder to find the real estate offer. My search was futile, so I made a mental note to ask my father about it.

"Now, it will be such a waste of materials and time after I win this. And money. Frankly, it's disappointing on many levels. I thought…" His gaze held a sadness as it met mine. "I thought perhaps you'd take my position more seriously, but it seems I was mistaken."

"What position is that?" I snapped. *I could think of several positions to put him in…* I gripped the tablet tighter so he didn't see me stumbling under his smoldering stare. No, I had to keep the upper hand. "You're the competition. City zoning allows for multiple hotels to be within reasonable proximity to one another. In fact, your hotel is less than a half mile away? Why have a problem with *this* hotel specifically? Could it be because you know we're in a whole other class?"

A slight growl left his lips. "Just as stubborn as *Signor* Jackson… And missing everything!" He pushed back from the table and stood. "Tell your boss he has once again wasted my valuable time. I'm done trying to work peacefully with him. Now I'm going to pursue a more aggressive legal route."

"We look forward to hearing from you," I quipped. Usually, I'd have said something far more eviscerating, but the memory of Matteo's warm hands guiding me over his cock and the way he took total control over my pleasure… it all messed with my brain. *How can I be terrible to a man who has unlocked something within me?* I hadn't even realized he'd captured me. I'd rather have given in to that initial urge to drag him to the table.

I watched Matteo and his assistant walk out of the conference room, admiring the way his suit was tailored to emphasize his strong back. *Another point for Matteo.* I had no choice but to declare him the winner.

It seemed we wouldn't see one another again after all. No way would he want to repeat our evening now. What was done was done, though. Deep down, I'd felt a connection, and for a second, it had felt like lovemaking. Had he felt it, too?

After Matteo left with his team, I looked around at

mine. I'd had my staff attend the meeting for show—strength in numbers and all that. "I'm going to call Mr. Jackson and let him know how the meeting went," I said. "I will let you know if anything impacts today's schedule."

They shared a knowing glance that said *daddy's girl fouled everything up*. They packed up their laptops and left, probably as eager to escape as I was to be left alone. With the meeting out of the way, they could now go back to doing their assignments.

I took in a slow breath and then dialed my father's number.

"Is it done?" he asked. "Is Russo finally going to back off? I could use some good news."

"Well..."

"That sounds like the beginning of *bad* news." The speed at which his tone shifted made me feel like a child again.

I cleared my throat. "*Signor* Russo wants to pursue more aggressive legal action."

"Which is the last thing I wanted." He groaned. "Naomi, please, you need to end this. My local sources have said the protestors plan to intensify their efforts and go after our licenses and permits. No food or liquor license and we're toast. If there is enough civilian backing, the proposed second location will be dead in the water."

"I tried to be nice to him. I really did. He acted as though *we* would give him what he wanted and not the other way around." I pinched the bridge of my nose and closed my eyes. "The whole meeting was less than ten minutes long."

"He's so stubborn," my father grumbled.

I nodded, even if he couldn't see me. "He mentioned a real estate offer. Have you had a chance to review it? It might be best to review his offer rather than an extended legal battle."

"No! I am not selling to him. This will be the first of many hotels we build in Italy." The urgency in his voice alarmed me. When he spoke again, though, his calm had returned. "There has to be a much better way to end this. Do whatever you can, Naomi. You're a smart and capable woman. I'm sure you have some ideas." He paused. "The last thing I want to do is clean up your mess. Because that's what this is now—*your* mess. Your failure to sit with him for even an hour could have cost us everything."

His words stung me worse than a slap. But he was right. I couldn't deny that. The meeting had been pathetically short, and rather than try to build a bridge, I'd just about burned it down. For what? Lust? The last power move in the game Matt and I had started the night before? I needed to get my view back to the bigger picture and get my head out of my fantasies.

Fantasies… I could potentially use that.

"I'll think of some options," I said, a plan already coming to mind.

CHAPTER TEN

Matteo

Heartless. She was cruel, much like her boss. Of course, she'd read the situation and only focused on the fact that I owned a competing hotel, skipping all the other details, like the city council's actions and how this part of town was my *home*. My family had put its roots here centuries ago. *Centuries.* The land Cygnus Group had purchased meant more to me than a section of dirt to develop, a means of making money. Naomi only saw it as that—money.

I didn't know why that revelation disappointed me so much. We hardly knew one another. We certainly hadn't spoken of our ambitions or passions beyond what we desired in the bedroom. Only a night of fun—that was all it was meant to be. Perhaps a brief fling. Casual. Those sorts of details were supposed to remain vague. All the same, I had gotten a completely different impression of her personality. Driven, yes, I felt that. She knew what she wanted, and she took it.

Perhaps I was terrible at reading people after all.

After the meeting, I took a long walk through town in search of memories. So many fond experiences I wanted to recreate for the guests of my hotel. I wanted them to open their eyes to Italy, to breathe her in. I had hoped the walk would energize and inspire me so going to my lawyer would feel like a positive step forward. Instead, I was left disheartened. The realist in me knew Ephraim Jackson had the politicians eating out of the palm of his hand. No matter how many violations I tried to cite, he had a counter for them all. His paperwork was spotless, the loopholes nearly impossible to spot. But I would find them. Somehow. I wasn't giving up, but I couldn't deny the uphill battle before me.

From there, my day ran on autopilot. I went about business as usual, and I felt more like myself with each passing hour. Being in the office always helped remind me of who I was and how far I had come.

Nothing could cause me to stumble… except for the woman who knocked on my office door just as I was about to call it a night.

The sound startled me. I'd been seated at my desk, trying to decide where to get dinner. Before I could say a word, the door opened, and Naomi walked in with my assistant on her heels.

Naomi folded her arms in front of her chest. "I don't want to resolve our dispute through our attorneys."

CHAPTER ELEVEN

Naomi

Shortly after five o'clock in the afternoon, I arrived at the Hotel Vesta Roma. A long line of guests formed at the front desk, and an equally long line for the concierge stretched across the lobby. Not wanting to wait, I flagged over one of the bellhops and pulled him aside.

"Buona Serata. Do you speak English?" He nodded his assent and I continued. "I'm Naomi Martin. I'm looking for the executive offices. Where do I go?"

He looked me up and down, taking in my business attire, and gestured for me to follow. "Right this way, *signorina*."

I turned and walked behind the man to the bank of elevators. When the doors opened, we stepped inside. He waved a keycard over the reader and pressed the button for the eighth floor. He smiled and nodded before stepping off the elevator.

I breathed a silent sigh of relief as the doors closed. I was one step closer to my goal of changing Matteo's mind.

The elevator carried me to the top floor in record time.

The door slid open to a small lobby area. I stood at the reception desk for a few minutes before giving up. I wandered along a row of cubicles until I arrived at the only person in the office.

The young, dark-haired woman appeared startled at my presence. She looked up at me, her brows lifted in surprise.

"Hello, Miss. How may I help you?"

"I'm Naomi Martin. I'm here to speak with *Signor* Russo."

"Do you have an appointment?"

"No. This is a follow-up to this morning's meeting with Cygnus Group."

She narrowed her gaze and picked up the telephone to call either Matteo or hotel security. I needed to make a move. I breezed past her desk toward a mahogany-stained door which I assumed was Matteo's office.

"Miss, you can't go in there!" She shouted after me.

My heels clicked across the marble floor. "Watch me."

I knocked out of courtesy. That seemed to be the least I could do, but I didn't wait for an answer. If Matteo ignored me, security might catch up and drag me out, and I wouldn't give him the satisfaction of watching that… not if I could help it, at least.

His administrative assistant was quick on her heels. She'd caught up with me just as I'd opened the door.

Matteo stood from his desk and seemed to waver between shock, awe, and annoyance. After telling him we didn't need attorneys, he turned his attention to the brunette standing alarmingly close to me. The two spoke in Italian while I tried to figure out what they were saying. She'd likely called me a rude, crazy woman and asked if she should call security.

He took a seat in his chair and raised a hand to diffuse her anger. As if on command, the administrative assistant stepped back and closed the door behind her.

I ignored his gestures to sit in one of the chairs and pleaded my case. "You and I can reach an agreement ourselves. Our legal teams will spend countless hours and dollars to resolve a conflict that you and I could do in less than a week."

"Attorneys complicate matters." His words were careful and calculated, but encouraging.

I took a few steps closer. I gawked at the size and luxuriousness of Matteo's office. Man, I'd thought my father's was impressive. Matteo had far more space and a classier decor. Where my father liked to show off his wealth, Matteo took a quieter approach. In doing so, it was clear just how much more money Matteo had. Cygnus Group's corporate debt levels had increased with the new land acquisitions and construction on this project. We'd essentially put all our eggs in the hotel basket. Matteo owned restaurants, theme parks, hotel-and-restaurant supply companies, along with a brand of ultra-luxurious hotels and casinos across the globe. In other words, Matteo was more than wealthy. He could take us to court… and for a long time. The fees would probably be chump change to him, whereas a drawn-out case could inflict significant financial damage to our company.

All of that should have fueled my anger. Instead, it opened a new desire for the man. The money didn't matter to me. However, what he did with it spoke volumes of his character, that sexy confidence he'd displayed at the club last night… and in bed.

But I couldn't let him know how much he'd impressed me. I had to stay calm and collected.

I made my way to his desk, slowing my steps and adding an exaggerated sway to my hips. "Yes, they are messy. I'd much rather settle this in a more… organic way."

He pushed his chair back as I walked behind his desk. I casually sat in his lap and draped my arms around his neck. Much to my surprise, he didn't nudge them away. "Surely we can come up with a mutually acceptable agreement. A way for everyone to win? I like you, Matteo. Let me make you happy."

Just as I was about to lean in and nibble on his ear, he placed his finger over my lips. His touch was gentle, and his gaze held no judgment. If anything, that strange sadness from the meeting had returned.

What am I doing wrong now?

"Naomi… What are you doing?"

"Trying to please you," I purred.

He let out a breath. "*Mi scusi,* I meant why are you doing this? I know perfectly well what your intentions are. What

I don't understand is why you would stoop to this level to get what you desire."

I looked into his eyes. Of course, he'd caught on to what I was doing. Men like Matteo didn't earn their wealth by playing dumb. They were damn near impossible to play.

With a sigh, I brushed away a few loose curls. "Fine, you caught me. I tried to take the easy way out. A girl can dream, right?"

"Naomi, you're more than welcome to have your every fantasy fulfilled whenever you wish. However, it will not come at the cost of my letting your hotel open." He trailed a few fingers along my jawline. He slowly dragged his gaze along my hair and then down to my lips before returning to my eyes. We stared at each other, and I lost myself in his eyes. Framed by long thick lashes, they weren't the dark brown I'd initially thought. They were a warm chestnut with golden flecks dancing throughout the irises.

I held his gaze, relishing his touch. "I don't know. I'm sure there will be a way I can convince you to change your mind."

"Perhaps it is I who will change yours," he challenged.

"You can try, but on that issue, I'm a hard sell."

Speaking of hard… Matteo's arousal grew evident as I continued to sit on his lap. Just for fun, I wiggled my ass to see what kind of reaction I'd get.

Matteo didn't disappoint. A low groan slipped from his lips. "That only makes it more enjoyable for me."

I grabbed him by the shirt collar and pulled his lips to

mine. The kiss we shared sizzled, and I welcomed his playful tongue. The warmth of his mouth left me reeling and dazed. Just kissing him was enough to set me off. That, plus the feeling of his cock pressing into me, begging to be released…

"Tell you what," I whispered huskily. "Fuck me on this desk, and then we can discuss the terms of our arrangement over dinner."

"Straight to business," he murmured against my skin. "I accept the invitation."

I didn't waste any more time. My fingers sought his waistband, plucking at the button. My heart raced a thousand miles an hour as I lowered his zipper and sought out his glorious manhood. As I freed his cock from his underwear, I gave it a slow tug. He let out a low hiss—like a pressure valve, releasing his pent-up frustration. The energy in the room changed from a maybe to a definitive yes. Matteo was beginning to see things my way.

I hitched my skirt up and moved onto Matteo's gigantic desk, facing him, my legs dangling over the side. With his cock in his hand, he slowly rose from the chair. He rubbed himself, taking time to end each stroke with a flick of his thumb. I was mesmerized by the beauty of his move. On the surface, he appeared utterly calm. However, the tightening of his jaw revealed he was desperately trying to remain in control. Seeing him respond in that way was a major turn-on. I trembled with anticipation for what was to come.

His eyes drifted from my stilettos up the lines of my

legs and landed at my inner thighs. He pushed my skirt up to my waist. I leaned back, spreading my legs wide so he could see how wet and ready for him I was.

"Your panties seem to have gone missing," he whispered. He leaned down and opened a desk drawer. He tore open the foil package and slid on the condom.

Matteo moved closer until our bodies melted together. His hands gripped my ass as he slid his cock between my folds. My wetness coated his shaft as he rocked back and forth.

I took several deep inhalations in a useless attempt to catch my breath.

With the tip of his cock, he teased my clit before slowly entering. "*Come sei bagnata.* You're so soaked for me."

He moved in and out, at an unhurried pace. He lifted my legs to shift them onto his shoulders and turned his face to press a kiss to my inner ankle. My God, he knew just the right way to position himself so he touched every pleasure zone. We pumped against each other, soft moans leaving my lips and words of Italian coming from his. *Il tuo corpo e' perfetto. Mi fai impazzire.* I didn't know what they meant, but they were by far the sexiest sounds he could have made. Nothing said *"I'm transfixed by you"* like being so far gone with desire you couldn't remember what language to speak.

Harder, faster, more urgently, we sought our ultimate release. I was first to arrive, my legs dropping to his elbows, spreading me wider for him. I didn't think it possible, but he reached even farther inside of me. My climax draining his cock paired with his solid, purposeful thrusts—they nearly had me seeing stars—were enough to bring him to a powerful orgasm.

His body shuddered, liquid heat warming me, and he leaned over me with his shaking arms supporting his weight. His breath came out in short pants. *"Stellina,* I look forward to this challenge."

CHAPTER TWELVE

Matteo

I watched as Naomi returned from my private washroom. Her skirt was short but appropriate, the hemline ending a few inches above her knees. Her amber-colored legs stretched for miles, ending in high-heeled shoes. My eyes followed along the curves of her body; I admired the way her business suit could make her a temptation while maintaining her professional persona. I couldn't say I'd ever met a woman like her. Yes, there were plenty of women who worked for me, but they all seemed to fall in one camp or the other—all business, taking on a more masculine approach to fit in amongst the men, or all play, having no problem using their feminine wiles for their advantage. Naomi did both so well.

"You understand nothing that happened here has made me change my mind," I said.

Naomi laughed. "How could I forget?" She fluffed at her hair as she gazed at her reflection in the window, reassembling her clothing and dabbing at her ruby-stained lips.

"Don't mistake my being easy to seduce as my being stupid, though. I know what I've gotten myself into."

With a smirk forming on my lips, I walked over to her and put my hands around her waist. I placed a small kiss on the space behind her ear. "One of the reasons I enjoy you so much. You're very intelligent."

Perhaps even *too* smart, so I would have to be extra careful. When I'd sought out Naomi for more of a challenge, I hadn't expected this much of one. I'd wanted a strong woman, someone who would attempt to dominate me, and then I would get the pleasure of putting her in her place again. Naomi would do more than attempt to control me. She'd succeed if I didn't keep a close watch on her.

That excited me all over again. She was dangerous. Very dangerous.

"Where should we eat? There's a great restaurant on the corner. The best chefs in the city," she said.

I scoffed, knowing the fancy establishment she spoke of all too well. It was where I had most of the meals with potential business partners. "Tables are near impossible to get."

"Good thing I have a great in," she said.

"As do I. I have also eaten my way through the entire menu. Sadly, over the years, their food has become more mass produced and less authentic."

She shrugged. "But the food is delicious."

"Oh, *Stellina*, have you forgotten why people like to travel the world and eat the finest cuisine? The purpose of what people like us do?"

"People see the world so they can escape," she said quietly. "And it's our job to provide our clients with the best one possible."

I stroked her back with my fingers. "There is much I need to teach you, I see."

"Teach me?" She chuckled. "Now I'm all kinds of curious."

"I know just the place," I said, ignoring her comment.

More importantly, I also knew just how I would win her and Cygnus Group's property.

CHAPTER THIRTEEN

Naomi

When Matteo said he knew just the right place to take me, I'd thought perhaps he knew of a quiet, upscale restaurant on the outskirts of town that had yet to attract a lot of attention. Some of the best gems of fine dining were the ones no one knew about and were awaiting discovery. I was excited when we arrived at a small eatery packed full of people.

Instantly, I felt out of place in my work attire. Despite Matteo also being dressed to impress, he seemed to blend in better. Then again, he also had a way of owning whatever room he walked into without even trying. He had respect as well as a captivated audience.

As we made our way to a table toward the back, he spoke in Italian to a few people we passed, greeting them like old friends.

"You're famous here," I said, moving to grab a chair. Matteo beat me to it and pulled it out for me. "Wow. So, chivalry isn't dead."

"Is there a problem?" Matteo asked, confusion on his face.

I sat, accepting his courteous gesture. "No. I don't want you to feel as though you have to treat me special. This isn't a date."

"Yes, I know. It's a dinner meeting."

"Exactly." I let out a soft breath of relief. The last thing I needed was for him to be smitten with me. If I were being honest, it might have helped me win him over with the hotel business, but broken hearts were nastier than lawyers. I liked this area of Italy and would likely visit annually for work. It'd be terrible to deal with any awkward tensions that might arise from such a breakup.

"So, I repeat, what's the problem?"

I smiled at him. "Not a problem but an observation. Pulling out my chair isn't something most men do anymore."

"You mean the *boys* you've dated?"

As I looked across the table at him, taking in that confident grin, I remembered again how much older he was. Twenty years, to be exact. Until that moment, it had been a minor detail I'd forgotten. After all, at the age of twenty-six, I considered myself an old soul. Age was nothing more than a number. My father was fifteen years older than my mother, and they were hopelessly in love.

At the club, he'd seamlessly integrated with others half his age. In the bedroom, he was a fucking god. Immortal, ageless. In the boardroom, he was my equal. Now, I could see the years of experience in his eyes.

It was sexy. I only hoped those old-fashioned principles didn't mean Matteo held antiquated gender values as well. Temporarily, I could suck it up for the sake of convincing him to give up on stopping our opening. Long term, however… *Wait, why even entertain that thought?* There was no long term. Our relationship was business, fun and temporary, nothing more.

After a moment, I relented. "Yes, the boys I've dated. Although you aren't the first man of your age I've been with."

"Do you prefer older men?"

"When they're like you, yes." I batted my eyelashes at him, teasing. "Most are just older versions of the boys. Which, I should add, isn't something I mind. It just keeps our trysts…" I struggled to search for the right word.

"Less gratifying," he supplied.

Our conversations are becoming too personal. Best to get things back on track. "We should come up with some ground rules for what we're doing, both on a business front as well as pleasure."

A waiter approached the table. He and Matteo had a lengthy exchange in Italian. The young man looked me over and then nodded at Matteo. I could make out "yes," but before I got a word in, he was gone.

I glared at Matteo. "What was *that* about?"

"Dinner."

"Did you just order for me?" I gasped. No man had ever done that before. Even my father. He was a controlling alpha asshole, but even he knew better.

He splayed his hands out in front of him. "To save us time."

"How do you know what I like?"

"I'm excellent at reading people."

I wanted to call bullshit, but I decided to wait until after the meal arrived to do that. For now, I would allow Matteo to live in his fantasy bubble. "As I was saying…"

"Yes, business, pleasure." He held the words, one in each hand, and pretended to measure them. "I want to continue to see you, to have you at my pleasure, for the duration of your stay."

"Even if things get complicated with the business side?" Before I agreed to anything, I had to make sure he understood he wouldn't seduce me into changing my mind. The fun would be watching him try but succeed in doing that myself with him, naturally.

He leaned across the table. "*Stellina*, whatever happens in our discussions will stay outside of the bedroom. I'm more than capable of separating the two."

"Good, because I am, too." I crossed my legs, shifting my weight. "All I ask is that when we do the business portion, you keep an open mind. Let me show you our hotel isn't so terrible. That it will help the town, grow it, and truly make it shine."

The waiter arrived with a bottle of white wine. He showed us both the label: a Frascati from a regional vineyard. So far, Matteo had a good feel for what I liked.

"*Grazie*," he said after the server opened the bottle and

poured the contents into our wine glasses. He then returned his attention to me. "Let me ask the same of you. An open mind. I will show you the true reasons the locals are protesting—to help you understand."

I lifted my glass to toast him. "Then let the games of persuasion begin."

"May the best man win." He clinked his glass against mine.

"Or rather, the best woman." I took a sip and grinned.

The server placed several steaming plates on the table. Matteo had chosen homemade tonnarelli carbonara and a shared platter of fried artichokes. I twirled a healthy forkful of pasta and lifted the utensil to my lips. My eyes rolled back in my head from the ecstasy of the butter-and-cream-ladened dish.

After we finished our main course, the server returned with a tray filled with a dessert flight. There were three small plates of panna cotta, tiramisu, and cannoli. Each dessert was beautifully displayed.

A terrifying thought washed over me—Matteo had read me perfectly.

I might have been in over my head.

CHAPTER FOURTEEN

Matteo

"Y ou attended college in the nineties. Wow." She widened her eyes and rounded her mouth into an exaggerated O shape. "Tell me… Did you use a computer or a typewriter? Or did you engrave research papers in stone?" Naomi laughed coquettishly.

"*Stellina*, you are not funny," I answered with mock seriousness. Wrapping my arm around her shoulder, I pulled her closer in the back seat of my car.

Our dinner meeting had been filled with pleasant surprises. Not only was Naomi charming, but she was well-traveled and socially conscious. She talked about how she had spent her summer holidays volunteering at Kenyan nursery centers and how she sat on a board for a college preparatory program for minority students. Her eyes sparkled as she talked about living in New York City—the museums and the best places to eat.

On the other hand, I told her how I took a risk in

attending Boston College and the culture shock of living in America.

We avoided all discussion regarding business.

We drank copious amounts of wine as the moon rose above the horizon. It had felt like a date. We had agreed that it was a casual business dinner. And yet, as I memorized each of Naomi's sexy mannerisms, I became entangled with her in ways that I did not expect.

When my car stopped down the block from her hotel, I exited and extended my hand to her. She reached out, grasping it as she climbed out. The protestors had returned to their homes and were likely spending a quiet evening with their families. She took a quick glance around the area before gliding in front of me. Seconds ticked by as we stared at each other in wonder. I felt the details of her life that she'd shared over dinner were just the tip of the iceberg. What were her parents like? Who were her friends? What did she like to do for fun? I needed to know every detail of her life—no matter how small.

Naomi stood on her tiptoes and whispered, "Good night, Matteo. Thank you for… everything." Her warm breath misted the outer shell of my ear. She pressed a hand above my heart before leaning in to give me the customary Italian greeting—a kiss on both cheeks. Her soft skin brushed against mine, and I took in a deep inhale. She smelled delicious. I imagined that she tasted the same: like late summer and wine—apples, limes, and grapes.

I wanted to dive back into the spontaneous whirlwind

of lust and sex that had permeated last night. I held her in place, pulling her close so she could feel my growing need. The flirtatious curve of her mouth told me that she had felt all of me.

"*Stellina*," I whispered, my voice gentle and seductive. "Would you like to go back to my apartment… for a night-cap? It's in the hotel."

"Thank you. But I'm afraid that I must take a raincheck. Jetlag has finally caught up with me. I need to be refreshed and ready to respond to any evil plan from a business rival."

I tried not to appear deflated, but her sexy smile wiped away all disappointment. I raised her hand, pressing it to my lips—a small gesture of thanks for the beautiful evening and an agreement for many more.

"I'll let you go if you promise to make it up to me."

She trailed her hand along the line of my cheek and jaw. She stared up at me, tenderly stroking my face with the pad of her thumb.

"I promise." With her free hand, she crossed her fingers then crossed her heart.

"*Buona notte, Stellina*."

"Good night, Matteo."

I watched as she strolled toward the bellhop stand. Her high heels sculpted her legs into perfection, and the sway of her hips was immensely tantalizing. I followed her until she disappeared into the building.

With a sigh, I returned to my car and sank into the backseat, already missing her.

Naomi's reaction to the restaurant spoke volumes about how little she knew of the town where she'd hoped to do business. She appreciated the culture, just like I thought she would. My instinct had been correct on a few things, but I'd been wrong about how to soften her up. Women who sought out casual relationships often did so because they had yet to be treated right. Naomi hadn't look pleased when I took control.

Funny, because she'd loved it when I controlled her last night… and earlier on my desk.

Perhaps that was the nature of our struggle. Power shifting back and forth constantly. I loved it. I shouldn't have, but I did.

I spent the rest of the night thinking about her as I closed my eyes and stroked my cock to memories of our bodies intertwined. My mind wandered to the black lace bra and matching panties that had emphasized her lines and curves and how beautifully she'd moaned. I wanted more, needed time to fully understand what made her tick. Time to show her all the places we would go—all the places we'd fuck—and how by the end of her stay, she'd succumb to my wishes.

I got started right away in the morning by calling her mobile bright and early.

"Ugh, hello?" she grumbled into the line.

"*Buongiorno*, I'm coming to get you in an hour."

"An hour is not enough time." She took in a slow breath. "How did you even get this number?"

"Your business card, where else?" I couldn't help but grin. "*Stellina,* an hour will be more than enough time. Our morning will include meals. Your beauty requires little effort. You will not need to dress up for this."

I imagined her narrowing her gaze as she lay in her bed. Did she wear sleeping attire, or did she sleep in the nude? The thought was enticing enough for me to consider putting down the phone and walking over to her hotel for a proper good morning. I resisted the urge despite the discomfort of my growing erection. Soon enough. I'd get to be inside her. Soon enough.

She gave me a terse "fine" before hanging up. We agreed to meet at the local market, and an hour later, she arrived, large dark sunglasses hiding her beautiful eyes. Even in her jeans and a loose-fitting crop top, she oozed the same appeal than as if she'd been wearing a tight, sexy dress or business suit.

"Okay, I'm here. What are we doing?" She shoved her hands into her pockets.

I walked over and kissed both of her cheeks before putting an arm around her waist. "It's time you see *my* Italy."

CHAPTER FIFTEEN

Naomi

The way he said those words, *my Italy*, gave me shivers. In his gaze was an intense determination. I wasn't quite sure what to expect. Still, I wish I had put a little more effort into my look because Matteo wore a navy blue fitted polo shirt, khaki pants, and leather loafers. The short sleeves emphasized his arms, drawing my eyes to the veins and sinewy muscles beneath his golden skin.

The late summer breeze blew through his hair as he guided me down the street at a leisurely clip. He pointed to a bakery that sat at the corner of a busy intersection.

"That café has the best espresso in all of Rome. The shop owner is very kind. He's an American who learned the fine art of the Italian roast at the hand of the masters. I'll take you there for breakfast one day." He stopped and looked up and down the street. "When I was a young boy, this thoroughfare was my playground. I sold treats, shopped for groceries for neighbors, and walked dogs. Anything to make spare change. I wanted a video game console." He chuckled. "Tell me about your childhood, *Stellina*."

"It was a regular childhood in New York City." I shrugged, shoving my hands in my pockets. "I'm an only child. I was artistic and inquisitive. I enjoyed exploring museums and doing arts and crafts."

I deliberately left out the parts about the Upper East Side brownstone, private school, and the beachside summers in Sag Harbor.

"And what are your parents like?"

My heart raced. I wasn't prepared to share any details of my life.

"My mother is a housewife. She's warm and caring. You would like her, and she would *love* you. My father works at the family business."

"What about your father? Would he not like me?"

"No comment." I nudged him with my elbow and laughed. He joined in, taking me by the hand, entwining his fingers with mine. We continued our leisurely pace down the cobblestone-lined street, not acknowledging that we were holding hands.

A thrill rushed through me. I looked up at the surrounding architecture, pretending to be interested, hoping my excitement didn't show. By all outward appearances, I was cool, but inside I was a giddy mess.

Matteo took me all over town. We visited every market, every small shop, basically every local business that we could pack into one day. Everyone knew him, loved him, and respected him. I smiled, watching their body language as they talked. I didn't speak enough of the language to engage in any conversations. The gelato shop owner gave us generous samples of the newest flavors. Matteo animatedly negotiated with the jewelry shop salesperson over the price of a lovely mother-of-pearl pinkie ring. The owner of a bread cart gave us hearty samples of baguettes and olive oil.

In the evening, he rewarded me with a single red rose and the best foot massage I'd ever had, followed by more mind-blowing sex. When it came to worshipping me, he did it well.

But I didn't drop my guard. I'd held his hand, took in the sights, absorbed the town and the people who lived in it, and my mind remained open as I promised. Whatever his goal was in showing me all of this, though… that was the mystery I hadn't quite figured out.

After a few days of exploring with Matteo, I received a phone call from my father.

"What's going on over there? My lawyers told me the protestors have backed off," he barked. No "*How are you doing?*" or "*Thank you for stopping the citizens from going after our business.*"

I rolled my eyes because I could get away with it. Normally, I wouldn't dare be so crass with my father. "We're negotiating, me and *Signor* Russo." Yes, that was the best way to word things. What Daddy didn't know wouldn't hurt him. "I've been meeting with him every day hoping to convince him to back down. At the moment, he's very con-cerned about the locals who live here."

"Of course he is." There was a grit in my father's voice I didn't understand. "A daily meeting about said locals seems unnecessary and excessive. I need you to take a firmer ap-proach. Stop playing nice with him! We have little time left."

"I know. The grand opening is coming up quickly. The inspectors are due in six days," I said. "But if it saves us a lengthy battle that could throw everything off schedule, playing nice might be better."

"Naomi…" he growled.

Before he could say another word, I added, "Playing nice gives us more wiggle room with the final permits. Surely there's something in them we can throw at Ma…*Signor* Russo to make him back down for good." Hopefully, that would be enough to calm him. "Surely, our legal team can come up with a strategy."

"Yes," he said after a long silence. "I suppose keeping Russo happy has worked to our advantage in some ways. The protests have stopped. He's been too busy meeting with you to go to the city with his demands. Again."

Oh, I've been keeping him busy. "Exactly."

"Try to get a solid resolution," he stated. "I'll be flying out there soon enough for the ribbon cutting and there's talk of receiving a plaque from the mayor."

"All right." What else could I say? We hung up shortly after, and I placed my phone back in my purse just as Matteo arrived at the coffee shop. Today, it' was my turn to show him a few things.

He reached for my hand and brought it to his lips, never taking his eyes off mine—a greeting he'd started giving me yesterday. This kiss wasn't the traditional Italian cheek kiss or the way one said hello to someone they dated casually. It was charming and so romantic. It put me on edge every time. Even more so when I realized I could get used to him kissing me like that. I'd never tire of it, and once our arrangement ended, I'd miss those kisses… and miss him. A lot.

The more time we spent together, the more my soul connected with his. Whether or not he meant to, each trip we took into town, he showed me more and more of the Matteo hiding beneath the surface. The man who was so much more than "business as usual." It felt unfair of me to withhold the fact that I was the daughter of his enemy.

That dilemma must have shown on my face because he frowned a little. "Is everything okay, my *Stellina?*"

"Yes," I said, smiling. In truth, no, things were not all right. *I could fall in love with this man, and I'm already in love with this town.*

Matteo was winning our game, but this wasn't the part that upset me.

If Matteo won, the game would end, and so would we.

CHAPTER SIXTEEN

Matteo

Something had changed inside Naomi. She was usually filled with confidence, but when I entered her room, her demeanor was far more pensive. As we toured the grounds of the hotel property, she had little enthusiasm. From our previous conversations, I knew she had been looking forward to this day.

"As you can see, the garden will inspire peace and relaxation in our guests," she said. She made a weak gesture to the beautiful flowers growing in the courtyard as we made our return to the lobby.

I stepped closer to her side. "*Stellina,* where is your fire?"

"I… it's still there!" None of it convinced me. I expressed this in my pointed gaze. When she looked into my eyes, she at last relented. "Your Italy is amazing. What you've shown me is incredible. I don't understand why we have to be at odds with one another, and it's… it's hurting me here." She tapped the left side of her chest. "Why can't what I do, what *I* love, be a part of what *you* love? There's been so much of a fight. It can't be the invitation of tourists into the town. You own a hotel, a few of them, if I remember correctly."

Slowly, I nodded. "This is my home. The men and women you have met are a part of a community who'd helped raise me when my grandmother, Fabiana, became too burdened with the task after my parents passed."

Naomi sat down on a bench, her expression sobering. "How young were you? If she had to raise you, then…"

"Ten," I said, taking the space next to her. "My parents were musicians. One dark and rainy night, they were driving home from a show. Their car skidded on the road and hit an embankment. They were both killed. Please, don't focus on that. It was sad, and it took me decades to come to terms with it, but I have. With the blessing of my family, I opened the hotel I own. Yes, there are plenty of others in the area or nearby as well. It's not that your company wishes to be a part of the community that troubles me. I can handle the competition. The problem is with *how* you're choosing to insert yourself into our lives."

Her eyes held confusion. She still didn't understand, and I was running out of ways to show her. That hurt me more than I thought it would. Not because I would lose the challenge. Games were fun and winning meant protecting my home.

"My work is my life," she said. "Something I think you feel the same way. I believe in the importance of getting away and seeing how big the world is. Your Italy is a great place to escape to, and I've worked hard on this hotel. I can't give it up."

"And I promised my grandmother I would take care of her. When I failed to do so, I vowed I would take care of the people here instead."

She frowned. "Failed to do so?"

"*Stellina*, the people that I've introduced you to were there when I needed them most. They are more than shop owners or employees. They are the life blood of this town. When Cygnus Group comes in and offers below average wages, then it's my responsibility to advocate for the citizens. They are concerned about their quality of life once they are no longer capable to provide for themselves. Many will be forced to either become reliant on public assistance and housing. Or worse, shipped off to live with their loved ones. They are concerned about their children's future. When your company came in and mesmerized the city council with your fancy dinners and golf outings, you establish a precedent which makes it harder on the everyday small business owner and worker."

"Matteo, those things are common. In America, most deals are made on the golf course."

"That's not how we do things in Rome. What drew you to Cygnus Group?" I asked, genuinely curious, and perhaps her answer would shed some light on what made her tick. "You've worked your way through the ranks quickly there, it seems. your boss puts a lot on your shoulders, and I know he isn't one to share power."

Naomi gazed into my eyes and tantalizingly nibbled on her lower lip, clearly torn between answering the question and pressing me for more family stories. I wanted to kiss those lips and ease whatever burdened her. "All my life, I've known that my destiny was to work in the hospitality industry. Specifically, to make sure our guests only have the best. And I knew I would do it at Cygnus Group. My… Mr. Jackson has taken it upon himself to groom me for more. I'm eager to learn and have those greater responsibilities. He's the first person who ever believed in me."

"My *Stellina*. Come back to my apartment," I whispered into her ear.

She nodded, and soon after, we took off for my hotel. We walked the eight blocks in silence. Once we were in the safety of the elevator, I reached for her hand. I intertwined my fingers with hers, tracing slow circles over her thumb with my own.

Once inside my suite, she lowered my zipper and snaked her hand inside. She found me stiff and ready. I closed my eyes tightly when she freed my cock and wrapped her hands around me, giving my arousal a slow, sensuous stroke. Her thumb brushed over the tip, spreading the bead of fluid over my tight skin. With her other hand, she pushed me until my back landed against the door.

A sly smile played on the corners of her lips. "Matteo,

have I ever told you that your dick is perfect?" She gave me one good caress before sinking to her knees.

She took me in her mouth, her tongue running along the underside of my shaft, not stopping until she took it all. She lavished attention on every centimeter, even puckering her lips around the head at the end of each lick.

She was Venus herself in modern form—the daughter of the god in the sky. A tawny-hued feminine deity who was the authority on wanton sexuality.

Naomi looked up at me, and our eyes met. Popping off, she smiled up at me. "Don't be gentle. Take my mouth." The restraints were removed, and I became a wild horse. I bucked my hips, wanting to be buried inside of her. I threaded my fingers through her curls, holding onto her scalp and guiding her movements and speed. I leaned my head against the door, biting down hard on my bottom lip, fighting the urge to release in her throat.

Naomi had a mouth on her. She was sassy and funny. Also, she knew all the little ways to make me feel good.

My eyes rolled back in my head. Everything went dark as I thrust into her—my hips worked with a mind of their own. I pulled back when I began to get close. She caught her breath before pulling me in again.

I was the luckiest man alive. An attractive, business-savvy woman knelt at my feet with her skirt riding above her thighs. Her usually bright eyes were heavy lidded, clouded with lust, as her hand slipped beneath the lace of her panties.

Caught up in the sensations and trying my hardest not to explode in her mouth, I uttered absolute nonsense. I think the words *"Be mine. Stay with me."* slipped from my lips. She paused, a tiny break in our carnal activities. Our eyes made contact, and her face indicated she had heard me speak the phrases. I silently cursed to myself as the weight of my words sank in. Naomi's expression softened and then she resumed going down on me. I pushed aside my admission, closed my eyes, and rode out the waves.

A long, deep groan escaped from the pit of my stomach, and I hurriedly pulled out. My cock pulsed as I painted Naomi's lovely lips with my cum, marking her as mine. And like a very good bad girl, she licked away every drop.

I tucked myself back into my pants and slid down the door until I was seated next to her. We sat in silence while our heaving chests and breaths slowed down to a normal pace.

"That was hot," she said, a self-satisfied smile on her lips. "You're even more beautiful when you come."

I stared at her seated next to me. Naomi's hair was mussed, and her lips were swollen from our activities, yet she was still the most gorgeous woman in this world. I trailed my fingers into her dark hair and twisted a stray curl around them gently. *An attractive woman who possessed charm and intelligence? How did I get so lucky?*

"You are beautiful with that lipstick smeared across your mouth. *Stellina,* what is it you say? *Sorry, but not sorry.*" She laughed at my imitation of her voice. I reached out and rubbed my thumb over her lips before taking her mouth.

I kissed her until I'd had my fill—unsure what my life would be without her.

CHAPTER SEVENTEEN

Naomi

A tiny voice in the back of my head had warned that one or both of us would develop feelings. Matteo had taken me by surprise when he'd breathed out, *"Stay with me."* An eternity had passed as the remains of his words floated between us.

The idea of spending a few more weeks with him sounded fantastic but wildly impractical. One-night stands rarely turned into full-blown relationships. Besides, I lived and worked four thousand miles away. We might have started off strong, but over time, the distance would surely kill our affection. Then there was this selfish part of me that couldn't bear the thought of Matteo finding happiness with another woman.

Instead of opening up and communicating my thoughts and feelings, I swallowed the words down one by one and stored them under lock and key.

We were at a comfortable stalemate with our business dealings. I'd given up on trying to persuade him that our project was good for the town. On the day of the hotel tour, I'd learned one thing: No matter how many great things my business could provide the town, it would never be good enough. When my father arrived to deal with the last of the paperwork, I'd tell him I did my best to persuade Matteo, but he just wouldn't budge. Hopefully, my father and his legal team had found a strong enough strategy to shut the dispute between them down for good.

Guilt gnawed at me as I walked into Matteo's office. I yearned for him, body and soul. In our game, there would be no winner or loser. One of us was bound to walk away. Why couldn't we have found a way for all of us to be happy?

There were a few more days left in my visit, and after that, Matteo would never want to see me again. Sure, he said he could separate business and pleasure—an easy lie to tell. I was sure Matteo had believed it the moment the words left his lips. He'd be bitter, though. Men didn't take to losing well—especially men like him.

"*Stellina.*"

I'd really miss hearing him call me that.

I said nothing back. Instead, I walked over to him and grabbed him by his shirt, much like I had the first time we'd had sex in his office. I figured that it would be the last time we kissed, so I had to make it a good one.

My hands roamed over his chest and up to the nape of his neck, pulling him closer. Matteo took control, moving his hands over the back of my neck, and then kissed me gently. He slowly traced a line of kisses down and back up my neck before returning to my lips. I opened my mouth, running my tongue along his bottom lip, a silent request to open for me. He chuckled, maintaining a firm but locked lip seal.

I didn't want a nice, sweet kiss, I wanted one that would rock my world.

I'll show you who owns this mouth, signor.

With my other hand, I grabbed him by his belt loop and pulled him closer. I nipped at his lip, taking him by surprise. His mouth popped open, and I stuck my tongue inside.

This time it was my turn to chuckle. My celebration was short-lived, though, as my mood turned lustful. His hands wandered down the sides of my torso. Lower and lower, until they were under my skirt. With his fingers, he delicately teased my pussy, knowing just the right way to get me excited. And he knew just how much so. It was obvious, I was sure.

"*Nemmeno immagini cosa ho intenzione di farti.* That means 'you can't imagine what I'm going to do to you.' You're so wet for me," he murmured.

My breath hitched. I hated that a couple of Matteo's fingers had so much power over me. A few strokes could ignite me internally with such an unquenchable desire. Not just for his body, but for the soul that lived within it. Matteo had indeed proven to be my perfect match in every way. The thrill of the challenge and the way he made my defeat taste so sweet. "Take me, Matteo. Please. I don't want to wait any longer. Take me and make me come."

Begging wasn't usually my style, and he knew it. A

satisfied smirk formed on his lips, and it turned me on far more than I wanted it to. After all, arrogance shouldn't have been sexy. It disgusted me so much in other men. I supposed that was because they lacked something Matteo had: compassion. He had the power. We both knew it. Yet he wasn't lording it over me.

"What if I want to make you wait, *Stellina*? What if I want to watch you squirm?"

Make me squirm? I'll make him!

I reached for the buckle of his pants and ripped it open. Before I could make another move, he brushed my swollen clit before putting one finger inside my wet channel. With his other hand, he undid the buttons of my blouse and unclasped my gauzy demicup bra, freeing my breasts from their confinement. He brought his lips over one of my nipples and swirled his tongue around it, laving it generously.

"Sir, I told you, you can't just—" Matteo's administrative assistant shouted from her desk. There were a few insistent knocks before the door burst open. I barely had enough time to process what was happening.

"Ah, Russo, it appears that you have lost," a recognizable voice gloated.

I got just enough of a glance to see the familiar frame of a tall man with skin the color of almonds barge through the door. His appearance was unusually casual, not his typical polished appearance. He wore a wrinkled white linen dress shirt, which was unbuttoned at the neckline, and there were faint fold lines on his slacks as if he'd left the airport and come directly here.

My father. Oh. My. God… I fumbled to return my breasts to where they belonged. I quickly turned my face away from the scene and lowered my gaze to the ground. *Maybe he'll walk out once he sees what we were doing. Perhaps he won't recognize me. Maybe…*

His laugh echoed through the room. "Oh, this is classic. You're busy with an intern, I'm guessing? Someone eager to reach the top. That's how you do things here, yes? Or so I've heard."

Ouch. The comment stung me. I knew Matteo liked no-strings-attached relationships, so the idea didn't surprise me. What did, however, was my father's assumption that any woman caught with Matteo was only using him. It felt like more of an attack against *me* than Matteo. Since when was he so misogynistic?

"Wait… Naomi?" Disbelief filled my father's voice, and he stormed across the room. The next thing I knew, he drew back his arm and punched Matteo in the jaw. The sound echoed through the room, ricocheting off the walls. "How *dare* you lay your hands on my daughter!"

Matteo stumbled back from the blow, a hand covering his face where my father had hit him. He clenched his free hand into a fist, and I worried he'd punch my father back. I was positive the thought crossed his mind. Instead, he shifted his gaze to me, and I had to look away.

"Dad, what are you doing here?"

"What am *I* doing here? What are *you*…?" He scoffed then. His dark-brown eyes narrowed into slits, revealing the anger boiling beneath the surface.

I risked a glance at Matteo. His gaze held a mix of shock and anger. "I'm Naomi *Jackson*. Martin is my professional name. Matteo, I swear, it's not—"

"What I think?" Matteo supplied, venom dripping from his voice.

"You said I was better than going that route," I reminded him.

My father laughed, the sound sour and hard. "Which is why you're half-dressed right now?" Before I could defend myself to either of them, he grabbed me by the upper arm and yanked me off the desk. "I'm disappointed in you, Naomi." He glared back at Matteo. "That's why I came here. To inform you that the final permit has been approved. It's done. We'll open in three weeks, and there's nothing you can do about it."

"To gloat," Matteo sneered. He shook his head as he gazed at me. "Your father…"

My father took me by the arm and pulled me over to the door. I tripped on my heels as he dragged me across the room. He leaned in and said, "When I told you to do what was necessary to convince Russo to back down, I didn't think you'd take *this* path. Go back to the hotel and await instruction." He opened the door, practically shoving me out before slamming it behind me.

Matteo's administrative assistant stared at me with wide

eyes. I held my head high and checked the buttons on my blouse, despite the feeling of dread churning my stomach. No way would my father ever let this go. More importantly, Matteo hated me. I would never be able to redeem myself, even to keep him as a friend.

I cried the entire way back to my hotel. Tears of shame slid down my cheeks. I'd lied to Matteo, I didn't have the guts to stand up for myself, and I could have lost something beautiful.

By the time I got back to my hotel, Salvatore and one of the bellhops stood outside of my door with a luggage cart.

"What's going on, Salvatore?" I asked.

He gave me an apologetic smile. "We were told to assist you with your bags. I've arranged a driver for you to the airport."

I pressed my lips together. *Of course, Daddy needs me as far from Italy as I can get. The corporate jet will be gassed up and ready to take off by the time I arrive.*

I pulled out my phone, debating if I should text Matteo and try to smooth things over before I left. At the very least, let him know I would no longer be there to cause more problems. Instead, I tucked it back into my purse.

We'd speak again, but only after I made things right.

CHAPTER EIGHTEEN

Matteo

Her *father.*

It explained so much, and I was an idiot for not putting the pieces together. *Why didn't I bother to learn more before becoming so entangled in her? I could've had someone else do it for me instead.*

The foolish, romantic part of me had thought I could charm all her secrets free from the tight clutch she held onto them with. No wonder she had never let herself become vulnerable.

I glared at Ephraim Jackson as I rubbed the spot where he had punched me. Pain radiated throughout my jaw and temple.

"Russo, you put your fucking hands on my daughter. My only child. Lucky for you I'm not the man I used to be. They'd be wheeling you out of here in a stretcher."

Big talk from a little man.

"This isn't what it looks like."

"Didn't I just see you doing Lord-knows-what with

Naomi? It doesn't matter because you will never see her again. I'll make sure of that." He tossed his head back, laughing maniacally. "You've lost two things today: the hotel site and my daughter. And on top of that, you got your ass kicked."

I growled, a warning he should not push his luck. "Naomi was the only reason I didn't kick *your* ass. She's gone now, so there's nothing preventing me from wiping that smug expression from your face."

Signor Jackson chuckled. He checked his reflection in the window, straightening his shirt.

"This ends now. No more protests. No liquor license violation reports." He paused for a minute. "If you decide to run for mayor, I'll make a contribution. Until then, I'll leave you to your thoughts." His tone was gleeful. He seemed to take delight in my pain. He walked over to the door and placed his hand on the doorknob. Jackson saluted with two fingers and walked out the door. I watched him until he disappeared from view.

I pulled a bottle of water from my refrigerator and sat in my chair. I placed the bottle on my chin, and relief slowly replaced the pain in my jaw, but not in my chest.

My phone rang, and I would've ignored the call if it hadn't been from my assistant. "*Signor* Russo, I just got word from the city the permits have been—" George spoke in a frantic voice.

"Yes, I know," I growled, my body still hot with rage. *Had that been Naomi's plan all along? To keep me busy while her father worked behind the scenes? Are they going to laugh about how they screwed me over in such an incredible fashion?*

"Our lawyers have done some research. We can continue with the protests and report any violations—"

I groaned as my face throbbed with pain. "No."

"No?"

"No." I sighed. "It's over."

"But—"

"I know," I said, not wanting to hear him remind me of the promise I'd made to my grandmother. "There is nothing more we can do. Even if we appealed, we would lose. Ephraim Jackson has his claws in too deep, and he has covered his tracks far too well. I will find another way to fulfill my vows."

Or I hoped so, at least. Only time would tell. If the situation served as a reminder of anything, it was this: Getting emotionally involved always ended badly. I was such a fool. I'd had hope when her eyes had lit up from our time together. She'd appeared to be a woman who wanted to better the world, not someone who thrived on the almighty dollar.

By being so caught up in our game of persuasion, I had lost sight of the goal.

I spun my phone on the desk with one finger before I picked it up. I scrolled through the recent calls on my phone until my thumb stopped on Naomi's name. It hovered for a second as I decided if I should call. When the screen went dark, I put the phone down.

"You won, Naomi," I whispered.

CHAPTER NINETEEN

Naomi

The plane ride home went far too slowly. I stared out the window, absentmindedly turning the ring I'd purchased the day Matteo showed me his Italy. Thoughts of him ran sprints around my mind. The traces of our last kiss still sizzled my lips. The lingering warmth of his touch heated my breasts.

As soon as I landed, I went back to my apartment and tried to wash all the pain inside of me away. No bubble bath or amount of alcohol was going to cure what caused me to ache. My father had conveniently placed me on leave for an unspecified amount of time. He'd asked me to review the events that occurred in Italy and decide if I was built for this job.

I liked Matteo, and the betrayal in his eyes as I left his office ate at me. I hadn't thought the approvals would come through so quickly. I should have, but I hadn't. It was almost as if they'd been fast-tracked. He'd distracted me just as much as I had him, it seemed. However, what destroyed me was how I felt as though I was missing a vital piece of information. Matteo's anger wasn't that of a man who had lost. No, it was that of a man who'd been betrayed.

The hotel had always been personal for him, and I never understood why.

In the weeks that followed, I constantly thought about it, trying to find the missing link. My friends dragged me to a local nightclub to let loose with them. I didn't bother with my usual slinky dress and heels but went with jeans and a T-shirt. This place had been my playground, but today I sipped on a cocktail at the bar. Lost in trying to figure out the solution to my miserable life, I was utterly oblivious to the men trying to make their move. None of them compared to Matteo, so I'd have said no anyway, but my sudden change in character concerned my closest friends.

"Don't look now, cute guy at two o'clock," Rachelle, my best friend from college, said in my ear.

I cast a discreet glance toward the dance floor. Two Wall Street types were standing at a cocktail table. The shorter one wearing a suit and tie winked at me.

"I'm good."

She leaned back on the barstool, bouncing along with the electronic beat and scanning the room for a guy that was her type. "Girl, what's going on?" Rachelle asked. Her exposed cleavage undulated as she shook her shoulders. "Because at least four guys have come up to you tonight, and you won't even look at them. What's up with the outfit? Why are you so covered up? Some wingwoman you are."

Rachelle and I had met our freshman year at Howard University. The first day, we'd discovered that we were two peas from the same pod. We were both from the East Coast and had somewhat similar upbringings. We were creatures of the night and enjoyed any activity that involved finding a man. She was the only person who really knew me.

Well, I guess I could add Matteo to that list.

"Not feeling the bar scene, I guess," I confessed.

"But why?" She gave me a pointed look.

That was the moment I knew I had to be honest with myself. Matteo had changed me, and God help me, I'd fallen for him. Like, in love. I wanted to see just how far we could go as a couple because I saw us going the distance, being more than what we'd pretended.

"Let's find someplace quiet to talk." I gave her an apologetic smile.

She shrugged it off. "The guys here have been pretty lame tonight, anyway." She winked. We quickly finished our drinks and said good-bye to our friends before calling a ride to take us to a nearby coffee shop. We ordered coffees and added a little bit of Amaretto from Rachelle's flask. In the coffee shop, I told her everything about my trip to Italy. Matteo, the mind-blowing sex, and my father's disappointment with me.

After taking a sip from her coffee, she let out a low whistle. "Wow, what a trip!"

"Yeah," I whispered.

"You're going to tell Matteo, right? That you weren't

trying to sabotage or use him. That you're interested in him?"

"I feel like he won't believe me, so what's the point?" I shook my head. "How do I make it better, though? Because… because I want him to have the property. It's important to him. More important to him, to the town, than what my father wants it for." Just thinking of Daddy made my blood boil all over again. "What do you think I'm missing? There's a reason Matteo hates him so much."

"There has to be someone who can explain. Friends? Neighbors? What about his employees?"

"George!" My eyes went wide. "George, yes, he would know! It's eight in the morning there. He'll be up." I sent him an email right away, asking for his telephone number. While I had been in the same room with George, I hadn't said two words to him, but he was Matteo's right-hand man, and I hoped he would provide some valuable information.

Sure enough, George didn't disappoint. I called the number provided, and he answered after two rings.

"Hi, George. I'm glad you took my call. I was hoping you could provide information on the land the Cygnus Roma Hotel resides."

"Yes. I'm happy to give the details. *Signor* Russo's grandmother owned an apartment building that sat on that spot. About fifteen years ago, it was torn down because of property damage caused by a fire. *Signor* Russo was low on cash and sold it to the city with a handshake agreement to get first rights to purchase. He wanted to build a nursing home there."

"My father purchased it from the city."

"Yes, and shortly after the property was rezoned to commercial without public notice or comment."

"Matteo was not happy about that."

"That's an understatement. *Signor* Russo fought it from the very start. He filed appeal after appeal and lost every time. The documents were either lost or ignored. He tried everything, but his efforts were futile. As a last-ditch effort, he made multiple offers to your father to purchase the hotel. Each offer higher than the one before."

"My father refused the offer because he wants to gain a foothold in that market." *But he also likes to make people suffer.*

"That's not the end of it. Three years ago, corruption rocked our town council. Bribes were accepted in return for helping advance business projects. We don't know for certain, but *Signor* Russo believes your father bribed the mayor and several council members to get the site rezoned," he stammered. "If it is determined that someone did take a bribe, your company will be banned from doing business here. I'm sorry to insinuate that your father is anything but ethical."

"No, it's fine."

"If you'd like, I can gather the city papers and send them to you electronically."

"Yes. That would be perfect. I'd like to ask you to send

them to my private email address." I paused, measuring my words. "How is *Signor* Russo?"

"He is very sad. He feels like a loser."

"I hate to hear that. I want to help. George, if you don't mind, I'd like to keep this conversation between the two of us. I hope you're okay with that."

"It's no problem."

"Thank you."

After exchanging good-byes, I hung up the phone.

"You're smiling," Rachelle observed.

I nodded. "Yup, I just learned the lengths my father is willing to go through to get what he wants."

"And that makes you happy why?"

I smirked. "Because now I no longer feel bad about helping Matteo get what he wants."

CHAPTER TWENTY

Matteo

Ephraim Jackson's hotel's grand opening was scheduled in a few weeks. Even the papers advertised the affair with promises of an elegant evening at the open house.

And then, overnight, the plans changed. Someone had removed the *Coming Soon* sign, as well as the Cygnus Group logo out front.

"New management," George said with a grin. "Someone heard about the protests and made Cygnus an offer they couldn't refuse. The site will remain zoned as commercial, but it won't be a hotel."

I gave a stiff nod, not as pleased as George apparently was. Ephraim Jackson didn't win. Perhaps something more beneficial would eventually open. "That's nice."

"That's *nice?* This is what we wanted!"

"What we wanted was to open our nursing home," I clarified. "But it's a small victory all the same. Whoever this new owner is, all the best to them."

"They're having a gathering with the community next week to—"

"Then I expect to hear all the details from you later," I said.

George frowned as we drove toward the outskirts of town. "Won't you come? I'd think you'd want to see for yourself what will happen in place of the hotel?"

"I have my own business to attend. It's time for me to move forward with my next project."

"The hotel in France," he said quietly.

"Yes, I've narrowed the location down to three places. I will spend the next two months away to soak up the local culture." That was how determining a building site should be done. "Perhaps when I return, I will feel ready to meet with the new owner. After that, we'll begin option three—transforming local politics."

George gave a quick nod and echoed my "yes." He opened his mouth as if he had more to say but then closed it.

The time away would give me a chance to nurse my wounds.

All the better. I preferred the silence. Walking away felt like I was quitting. Grandmother would've understood, though. Overall, she wanted me to pursue love and happiness. *My life is complete as long as yours is.* Those were the last words she'd said to me before I left on my trip.

While I wouldn't ever be truly whole again without Naomi, I would get as close as possible.

CHAPTER TWENTY-ONE

Naomi

I spent a week in a whirlwind of meetings with my wealth managers and attorneys. The consummate professionals showed no reaction when I explained the plan for my new venture.

After my legal team drew up the paperwork, I invited my father to my attorney's office. He swaggered into the conference room, glancing at the man seated at my side. My father tossed his leather portfolio on the table before sitting in one of the chairs.

It had been two weeks since the incident in Matteo's office. In those two weeks, I began to see my father with a new set of eyes. I still loved him, but his need to always win no matter the cost saddened me.

"Hi, Daddy." I greeted him brightly with a confident smile.

"Naomi, what's this about?"

"I want to buy the Italian hotel."

A slow smile spread across his face. He looked at my attorney. "I'd like to speak with my daughter alone."

My attorney turned to me, and I nodded. He gathered his iPad and exited the room.

"What's on your mind?" My father leaned back in his chair.

I pushed a file folder containing the offer to his side of the table. "I've prepared a bid for the hotel that's more than acceptable."

"I don't want to read about it. Talk to me."

"I'm going to open a senior housing building."

He raised his arms in frustration and rolled his eyes. "In Rome? Have you done any research on that?"

"Yes, I have."

"Why should I sell to you?"

This time I pushed another stack of papers over. "I figured you would ask that. Here are notarized affidavits from the Italian officials along with a copy of the indictment of the former mayor. Accepting money in exchange for services." I clicked my tongue, slowly shaking my head. "I believe you know him."

There was a subtle change in his expression, an acknowledgment that he'd engaged in deception to acquire the Roman property. Catching himself, he steeled his face and crossed his arms.

"Okay. What do you want?"

One hour later, I emerged from the conference room the owner of a brand-new mortgage. My father agreed to seller financing. For the next twenty years, I would make quarterly payments to Cygnus Group.

He was livid that I'd beaten him at his game. The last words he'd said were, "*The ATM is closed. I mean it. You'll regret this decision.*" Naturally, I disagreed. Was the bridge burned between us forever? Only time would tell, but I felt no remorse for fixing what he'd broken.

Rather than tear the building down and leave a hole in the ground to rebuild on, I planned to renovate all the hotel rooms into apartments for what would become Casa di Fabiana—the nursing home and assisted living facility I'd named for Matteo's grandmother.

There were so many things to do. Before I left New York City, I had a conference call with the hotel staff and practically begged them to stay on board. It was a humbling experience. Fortunately for me, there weren't many options in the local job market.

In addition, I had to hire nursing staff, nutritionists, physical therapists, and security. In the end, we found experienced and caring people to achieve my vision.

From there, I hired an assistant to sell and pack up my things in my New York City apartment. I filled two duffle bags with my essentials and set off for the most incredible adventure of my life. I moved into one of the long-term staff apartments in the building and planned to put my previous work experience to good use to make sure the residents had the best care possible. More importantly, the retirement homes would remain affordable, even if it meant digging into my own pockets for a while. I didn't mind at all. It would be a better use for my money than just letting it sit in an account and collect dust.

Even if Matteo didn't forgive me, I could at least give him a proper apology.

But he hadn't responded to my texts or emails. George mentioned that Matteo was scouting locations in France, so he had no idea what I'd done. I didn't give him any indication of my true feelings through those brief exchanges. If he didn't want to hear from me, then it was good to save myself the embarrassment of having him laugh in my face after I told him.

At least I had Rachelle with me to help. I mentioned that I needed an experienced accountant, and she'd had her bags packed before I'd even asked her to join my company. She was looking forward to the new adventure. She and George had been great at getting the new building renovations off the ground and finished in a timely fashion. We were scheduled to open in the next week.

"Hey, Rachelle. I'm starving. Did you find a table?" I spoke into my phone as I hurried to a taxi. The plan was to meet at the restaurant Matteo had taken me to on our first date. While the memory stung, I had to face it if I ever hoped to heal.

Rachelle chuckled. "Fat chance, but I got one at the restaurant down the block. I'm already sitting and waiting. Just give them my name when you arrive."

Disappointed, I took the cab over and gave the hostess

Rachelle's name. I was led back, but the table was empty. Assuming she was in the bathroom, I pulled out my phone and waited.

And waited.

And waited.

Maybe she'd fallen in or had been kidnapped.

As I picked up my phone to call her, a man approached the table and cleared his throat.

Even with my gaze on my phone, I knew who stood there.

Matteo.

CHAPTER TWENTY-TWO

Matteo

Naomi had returned. *Why?* I thought I would never see her again despite hoping I would.

"Hi," she whispered.

She gave me a weak smile, and I attempted to return it. We both glanced away for a moment.

"My friend and I are having dinner here and…" She stumbled over her words, which wasn't like her at all. My Naomi was confident. Perhaps that meant she felt genuine remorse? When I looked into her eyes, though, I saw so much pain. I wanted to kiss her and remind her just whom she had attempted to double-cross.

I waited too long to respond. "I'm afraid our meeting is no coincidence. George asked me to meet him here. Stopping by has been a mistake; I will not disturb you," I said and turned to go.

"Wait!" There was so much desperation in her voice. "Please, let me just say this first. I'm sorry."

With some reluctance, I joined her at the table. "Naomi, I got your messages."

"I couldn't properly convey everything in them. I was afraid to." She closed her eyes, took a deep breath, and then opened them again. "Because there aren't words that can say what I'm feeling. The *depth* of how sorry I am. I should've done more research, paid more attention to what you were trying to tell me about the hotel. George shared the entire story, and I was the one who bought the hotel from my father."

I frowned. "Why? You didn't know her."

"But I know you, and I know she was special to you. More importantly, you're special to *me*. Somehow in our time together, you've gotten me to fall in love with you, Matteo." She laughed and blinked away a few tears. "Love. I didn't think I'd ever feel that emotion. The thought of tying myself to anyone for longer than a few days scares the crap out of me. But I want that with you. Even though I know it's probably never going to happen. I want that *with you*."

Naomi poured her heart out to me, but I couldn't think of a word to say back. I was stuck on two things. First, she'd purchased that hotel from her father to make *my* dream come true. Second, she'd done it because she loved me. The last time a woman had said she loved me, it had been nowhere near this level. Naomi did it all with no guarantee that we'd be together. She acted without a personal agenda.

She loved me.

"What you've done…" I said slowly, searching for the words. "Thank you for righting your father's wrong."

Naomi exhaled, and she seemed relieved. "I'm so sorry. I really can't say it enough. If there's any way I can—"

I held up a hand. "No need for you to apologize. I need some time."

"Yes, of course," she said evenly. "I didn't mean to assume…"

Oh, how I wanted to touch her cheek and explain the reasons why. That it wasn't because I was still angry with her, but simply that I had to sort through so many feelings. We had stepped beyond casual. She had my heart, and I had to determine if she was allowed to keep it.

"Now I'm the one who is sorry, Naomi."

She waved a hand in front of her face. "I'm going to go." There was a quiver to her voice, and she stood up. "Because I'm going to cry, like full-on ugly cry, and I don't want you to see that. I don't want your pity; I'm just grateful I have your understanding. Thank you for that."

CHAPTER TWENTY-THREE

Naomi

And ugly cry I did. It wasn't something I liked to admit to anyone, but I'd promised myself I'd be honest with Matteo even if it killed me. I'd spent too long holding back for the sake of looking strong, and it had cost me everything.

The following morning, I felt hungover even though I hadn't had a drop to drink. When there was an insistent pounding on my door, I cursed whoever dared to intrude in such a rude fashion. Only an asshole would be so loud at seven o'clock.

Dread filled me as I realized that asshole could very well be my father, finally coming to chew me out and tell me how he beat me. Because that would be something he'd do. Find a way to hurt me back. He'd always been vindictive. I'd just never been on the receiving end of it.

I attempted to make myself look presentable and powerful before answering the door. I pushed my shoulders back and raised my chin, swinging the door open.

Matteo stood on the other side, his hand poised to knock again.

I gasped, and he crushed his lips to mine. His searing kiss felt like home.

We didn't make it to the bed. He shut the door with his foot and pinned me to the wall. I pulled down his sweatpants and my pajama bottoms, not giving him any doubt about how much I needed him.

"Please," I managed between kisses.

And he was more than happy to oblige. He wrapped my legs around his waist and plunged into me swiftly and powerfully. I inhaled at the intense, familiar pleasure that coursed from my clit, through my belly, and throughout my body. I wrapped my arms around his shoulders as I held on for dear life. He pumped against me with firm and powerful strokes, leaving no space between us. We were one, physically and spiritually. Whole.

Months of pent-up, unspoken words came out in that rough, raw moment. I cried out each time I came.

"*Mi amore*," he groaned at last, now spent. "*Sei tutto il mio mondo.* You're my world."

My heart exploded. Matteo was mine, and I would never let him go.

We lingered there for a few seconds, our eyes locked. With a smile, he carried me to the bed.

"I thought for sure you would have nothing to do with me," I said. "And I wouldn't have blamed you. Just the fact that you accepted my apology felt like a miracle."

He kissed my forehead gently. "At first, I thought I was only a conquest. That was what hurt me. I know we had said to separate business and pleasure, but our time together brought us so close. Only a callous person could've continued in such a fashion."

"And you thought I was that person," I whispered.

"No, I didn't," he said. "That's the thing. I have always known, even if you didn't. When your father came to my office, he caused me to doubt. I knew I had to see you again to know for certain. The fact that you did so much for me while expecting nothing in return is proof your love is real."

"Then why did you let me leave? Why didn't you tell me at the restaurant how you felt?"

"Once I knew you loved me, I had to be positive I loved you, too. I came to that realization far too late last night. Perhaps I should've told you then, but it felt cruel to bang on the door at three in the morning."

"I was awake." I kissed him softly on the lips. "What matters is you're here, and we're together." I laid my head on his chest. "You're stuck with me."

Matteo laughed. "That was the point of coming back. I need you by my side. I never want to feel the agony of your absence again." He kissed me again. "My *Stellina*."

EPILOGUE

Matteo
La Piazza del Borgo, Puglia, Italy

I leaned against the bar as I watched my blushing bride on the dance floor in the middle of the courtyard. Naomi spun like a ballerina, her white dress billowing around her. The purest joy radiated from her beautiful face as she held her father's hand and twirled.

The week after the grand opening of Casa di Fabiana, she'd stopped by my flat every evening for dinner. After a week, she never went home again. While she slept, I memorized the sound of her quiet little snores, envying the moonlight as it caressed her lovely cheek. I knew that my life would never be the same without her, and I would ensure she would never leave again.

I would've given Naomi the world, but I knew she wanted her father.

Four months after she moved in, I traveled to New York City for a business meeting. While there, I invited her parents to dinner at one of the finest Park Avenue restaurants. I sat at the white tablecloth-covered table, sipping on a bourbon and adjusting my cufflinks. When her parents finally arrived—twenty minutes late—I stood and straightened my back as if preparing myself for battle.

Naomi's mother, Josie, profusely apologized while Ephraim approached, with his usual conceited smile on his face. He didn't offer any explanation. Ephraim sat at the table and promptly ordered a drink. He spent the first course of dinner sucking back gulps from his glass and looking bored.

"It's a pleasure to meet you, *Signor* Russo. Naomi has told me so much about you." Josie had beamed over at me. Looking at Josie's face, the source of Naomi's beauty was evident. Josie was as youthful and vibrant as her daughter. They looked more like sisters instead of mother and daughter. The difference was Josie had a worldly air that Naomi hadn't yet tapped.

"The pleasure is all mine. Please call me Matteo. I'm traveling for business, but I wanted to introduce myself. I would like to put the ugliness of the last few years behind us."

Josie had eagerly accepted the extended olive branch, but Ephraim merely grunted a non-committal reply.

I hadn't thought of the impact this fracture in the father and daughter relationship would have on Josie. On a whim, her only child had packed up and moved to another country. I remembered my grandmother's tears when I boarded the plane headed to Boston for my first year at university.

I could only imagine the toll missing a child had placed on Josie. I hoped hearing about Naomi's transition to Italian life and how much I loved her daughter put her at ease.

"Italy has been good to Naomi. The nursing home is going strong. She's built a community. The staff are highly trained and treat the residents with dignity and respect. It is a fun environment—there are social dances and movie nights for the residents. She's become a local darling."

"That's wonderful. Naomi has always been a brilliant and creative girl," gushed Josie. "Ephraim, did you hear that? The nursing home is a success."

"How many Americans care enough to establish a social service in a small Roman suburb? Let alone when there are facilities needed *here*, in the United States. It's mere curiosity. Everyone's interested in the young, foolish American who built a nursing home." Ephraim smirked, leaning back in his chair and taking a sip of his drink.

The dismissive air of superiority in his tone infuriated me. I clutched my brandy glass tightly until my knuckles turned white. My *Stellina* had done well. Her father should have commended her.

"Oh, Eph. You don't mean that. Naomi's your mini-me. Smart, determined, and so confident." Josie turned her attention to me. "Matteo, those two had a special bond from the moment she was born. Ephraim took her from my arms and just stared at her in disbelief. He whispered a blessing before saying"—she put her knuckles on her hips and straightened her back, imitating her husband's speaking voice—"*'Josie, she's going to rule the world.'* It was so sweet and perfect. Naomi never left his side. They were so close. It was never any surprise when she went to work for the business. I used to be jealous of their closeness, but I wouldn't want it any other way."

"She is wildly gifted. Everything she touches turns to gold. My life is much more interesting with her in it." I pulled out my mobile and flipped through photos of our escapades: yachting on Lake Como, skiing in the Italian Alps, and hilariously posing in front of her new shiny red Vespa. It was impossible to ignore the love that shone brightly in each image.

Josie was brimming with excitement. Her daughter had taken a massive step toward living life on her own terms. Ephraim was unfazed by the photos and even less enthused about my love for Naomi.

"Matteo, I speak for Ephraim and myself when I say that we're happy our daughter has you."

"Josephine, please do not speak for me. I'll speak for myself." He said it firmly but softened his expression when he noticed his wife's disappointment. It was clear that Josie had him wrapped around her little finger.

I put aside my pride, took a deep inhale, and said the words that would change my life.

"There is something else I would like to discuss." I pulled the blue box that contained the engagement ring from my jacket pocket. I'd spent the morning at the Tiffany and Company store selecting a perfect diamond and setting.

The rush job had cost a small fortune, but Naomi was worth every penny. "Ephraim, I would like your daughter's hand in marriage. I'm passionately in love with her and will move heaven and earth to make her happy." While heartfelt, my request was not long-winded and held no hint of a plea. It was a sincere appeal from a man to his love's father.

I did it for Naomi.

The dinner to ask for her hand was an opportunity for Ephraim and me to move toward friendlier interactions. If he couldn't put our business conflict aside and denied my request for Naomi's hand, I would still propose to her. Together, we would work to repair their relationship.

Josie and I waited for her husband to answer. Josie's own hands trembled, tears filling her eyes, while I remained as cool as a cucumber.

Ephraim Jackson was a stubborn, egotistical bully, but he loved his daughter. He gulped back his whiskey on ice and reluctantly nodded his blessing. He extended a hand, and we shook like gentlemen. Josie rushed from her seat and wrapped her arms around his neck, smothering his face in kisses. That was the first time I had seen Ephraim Jackson smile.

The day after our engagement, Ephraim had sent a large floral bouquet, which prompted a telephone call from Naomi. The call led to Ephraim and Josie's two-week Italian holiday. There were several closed-door discussions between the three. Naomi never gave details about their conversations, preferring to say that her father apologized, and she accepted.

The second time I saw Ephraim smile was when the officiant pronounced Naomi and me as husband and wife.

She was the apple of her father's eye, but she would always be the star of mine.

I had not expected the marriage to thaw the iciness between Ephraim and me, but I hoped that time and grandchildren would begin a gradual warm-up. Maybe soon, we would break bread at an American Thanksgiving dinner or exchange gifts during *Natale*.

Ephraim showing up at the wedding had been a huge overture.

Familiar arms wrapping around my waist shook me from my memories. *"Buonasera.* I was hoping I'd catch you before you ordered a drink."

I looked down at my wife. Her eyes glowed with a mixture of love, excitement, and exhaustion. She had spent the last four weeks preparing for her closest friends and loved ones to travel to Italy for the wedding. I had suggested hiring a wedding consultant, but she had insisted on doing it herself. *"It's all about the experience, babe,"* she'd quipped.

A glinting flash on her hand caught my attention. She wore the only memento of my mother, a simple platinum wedding band, on her ring finger. Raising my head to the night sky, I whispered a hushed thank-you. I knew my loved ones had played a part in bringing us together.

"Is this your way of offering to pay for my drink? Or is it an invitation?"

"It's an invitation, of course. *Balla con me, amore mio.*"

Dance with me, my love.

Leaning in, I nuzzled my favorite spot at the base of her throat. I made animated chomping noises as I playfully nipped at her flesh, sending her into a frenzy of giggles. She tossed her head back and let out a loud laugh—a bubble filled with love and affection. Her lighthearted mood was girlish yet sexy. She was irresistible. And all mine.

I brought her hand to my lips, inhaling her sweet smell, before I pressed a small kiss on her skin.

"Lead the way, my *Stellina.*"

THE END

If you have a moment, please review *His Little Star* on Amazon, Bookbub, and Goodreads. Help other romance readers and tell them why you enjoyed the book.

OTHER BOOKS BY
MICHELLE KARISE

Kandi's Crush
It's a Work Thing

Coming Soon:
Charming Hotshot—A Cocky Hero Club Novel
One Tiny Kiss—A Big Easy Novel

Be the first to know about upcoming steamy
multicultural romance and fabulous giveaways? Sign up
for my newsletter at michellekarise.com/the-sweet-spot.

Check out my website for more details.
WWW.MICHELLEKARISE.COM

ACKNOWLEDGMENTS

To my family and friends: Thank you for understanding why I'm sometimes distracted. I love y'all!

TK Cherry: Thank you for the beta read and your invaluable feedback. I appreciate you!

Najla at Qamber Designs: Once again, you've spun magic. Thank you for creating such a beautiful cover and making the design process so easy.

Lauren and Janine at The Write Divas: Thank you both for adding sparkle to my words. Your feedback was not only informative but hilarious. I can't wait to do it again!

Stacey Blake at Champagne Book Designs: Thank you for the beautiful design. I look forward to working with you again.

Love,
Michelle Karise

ABOUT THE AUTHOR

Michelle Karise is a St. Louis native who lives with her temperamental Shih Tzu, Rooney. The sassy, Type-A personality is a member of several professional organizations, notably the Romance Writers of America.

Travel, martinis, and wit are her jam and nuance is her butter. She constructs sophisticated erotic romance featuring intelligent female leads and the confident and strong men that love them. Sometimes the hero and heroine don't behave in ways that please Michelle, but she's always optimistic that love will prevail.

Looking for more steamy multicultural romance?
Check out my website for more details.

WWW.MICHELLEKARISE.COM